Matt strained his eyes against the night.

The bait, a raw buffalo haunch, lay untouched next to the creek. It was rapidly growing too dark for decent shooting . . .

It came with a purr of sound and a whisper of movement, a leaping shadow. Kincaid rolled onto his back, realizing too late that the cougar had been on the ledge above, watching.

Matt tried to bring his Springfield up, and failed. The cougar collided with his body, smelling musty, its fierce, muscular body sprawled across his . . .

EASY COMPANY

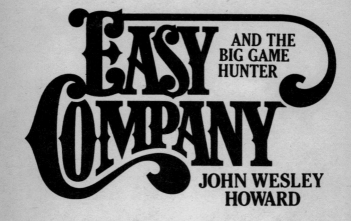

EASY COMPANY

AND THE BIG GAME HUNTER

JOHN WESLEY HOWARD

A JOVE BOOK

EASY COMPANY AND THE BIG GAME HUNTER

A Jove Book/published by arrangement with
the author

PRINTING HISTORY
Jove edition/May 1983

ISBN: 0-515-06360-6

Jove books are published by Jove Publications, Inc.,
200 Madison Avenue, New York, N.Y. 10016. The words
"A JOVE BOOK" and the "J" with sunburst are trademarks'
belonging to Jove Publications, Inc.

PRINTED IN THE UNITED STATES OF AMERICA

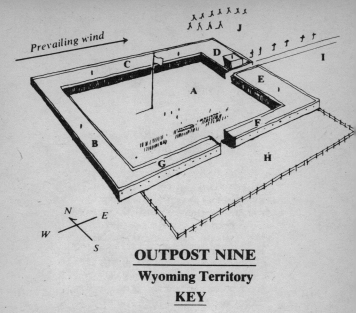

OUTPOST NINE
Wyoming Territory
KEY

A. Parade and flagstaff

B. Officers' quarters ("officers' country")

C. Enlisted men's quarters: barracks, day room, and mess

D. Kitchen, quartermaster supplies, ordnance shop, guardhouse

E. Suttler's store and other shops, tack room, and smithy

F. Stables

G. Quarters for dependents and guests; communal kitchen

H. Paddock

I. Road and telegraph line to regimental headquarters

J. Indian camp occupied by transient "friendlies"

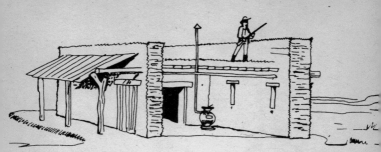

INTERIOR   OUTSIDE

OUTPOST NUMBER NINE
(DETAIL)

Outpost Number Nine is a typical High Plains military outpost of the days following the Battle of the Little Big Horn, and is the home of Easy Company. It is not a "fort"; an official fort is the headquarters of a regiment. However, it resembles a fort in its construction.

The birdseye view shows the general layout and orientation of Outpost Number Nine; features are explained in the Key.

The detail shows a cross-section through the outpost's double walls, which ingeniously combine the functions of fortification and shelter.

The walls are constructed of sod, dug from the prairie on which Outpost Number Nine stands, and are sturdy enough to withstand an assault by anything less than artillery. The roof is of log beams covered by planking, tarpaper, and a top layer of sod. It also provides a parapet from which the outpost's defenders can fire down on an attacking force.

one _____

The evening was cool and still. The deep skies were clotted with white stars. The tip of the rising crescent moon showed itself above the eastern horizon. The long grass waved gently in the night breeze.

She was warm and accepting. Her lips were pliant and searching as she dragged him down into the grass, her eyes wide, reflecting the starlight.

She was a strong and competent woman, fleshed out with long sleek thigh muscles, broad compelling hips, full dark-nippled breasts. She lay against the dark grass, her lips parted to reveal white, even teeth. Her hand snaked across Andrew Pettigrew's abdomen and slipped between his legs, and Pettigrew shuddered happily.

"Do me love, Andrew Pettigrew," the Sioux woman said, and Andrew Pettigrew obliged.

Dawn Fox was her name, and she was very young, handsome in the Sioux way, taller than was usual, with a prominent but attractive nose, deep, dark eyes, and long blue-black hair that just now was fanned across the grass as she breathed a little more quickly, her hand caressing Pettigrew, positioning him deftly.

"Do me love," Dawn Fox said again, settling back, her hands behind her head, her eyes watching the young soldier's face.

Pettigrew did her love. He slipped into her and lowered himself to rest his head against her breasts as she stroked his hair, and her hips, like restless, gobbling things, rose and fell, swaying from side to side, leading Pettigrew on a long, delectable journey into a soft and fluid land where all was warmth, long sighs, exquisite torture.

He kissed her breasts and became lost between them. His own body grew rigid, and his hand slipped beneath her smooth, firm buttocks, lifting her to meet him.

Dawn Fox was smiling. Her eyes were merry and distant. Pettigrew was watching her face, which seemed to go slack, to be softened with enjoyment. The sight of her enjoying him spurred him on, and he rushed toward his own completion as Dawn Fox's fingers found him and felt the eagerness in him, the final pulsing finish to their lovemaking.

They lay together quietly as the dew settled. Dawn Fox had drawn the blanket around them, and they were warm and cozy beneath it. They were the only people on the plains, the only people in the world.

"Andrew Pettigrew?"

"Yes, Dawn Fox?"

"My father wants to know about the ten horses."

"I don't have them yet."

"My father wants to know about them. He says that is the marriage price. Even though you are a wealthy soldier who gets silver from Washington, he says I must

2

tell you a son-in-law must be a man with horses. He says you must bring them soon or I will be given to Black Hatchet."

"That ugly bastard. That arrogant—"

"I hate Black Hatchet," Dawn Fox agreed. She propped herself up on one elbow, her breast falling free of the blanket to be painted with moonlight. "Yet this is the way it must be. My father says you must bring ten horses if we are to be married."

"I'll get them. Soon. I'll bring them to your father and we can be married." He bent his head to the escaped breast and kissed it. "Then, when I get my discharge, we can settle along the Heart River. I told you about that place." He nuzzled the breast again.

Dawn Fox pulled away a little. "But when, Andrew Pettigrew? I must tell my father. Have you asked your chief to give you horses?"

"Captain Conway?" Pettigrew laughed. He had a vivid mental image of himself asking the captain for ten army horses to give to Dawn Fox's father. "No. I can't do that." In fact, Pettigrew hadn't even spoken to the captain yet. He supposed he would have to do that. He didn't mean to wait until his discharge—two months away—to get married.

She was a lovely, sloe-eyed thing, this Dawn Fox. Pettigrew had met her in Tipi Town when he and some of the other men from Outpost Number Nine were searching for the renegade, Shell Eye, who was supposedly hiding out there. They never found Shell Eye, who was in fact a hundred miles away, butchering a sodbuster and his family, but Pettigrew had found Dawn Fox.

"I must go." She smiled, touched his cheek with the back of her hand. Then she raised his hand and kissed the knuckles one by one.

"Tomorrow night?" Pettigrew asked hopefully.

3

Dawn Fox shook her head. "I cannot, Andrew. My father did not want me to see you tonight. The horses—" She leaned forward to look into his eyes. "You must soon get the ten horses."

"I will," he promised her, and Dawn Fox smiled brilliantly. She slipped into her buckskin dress, paused to kiss the top of his head, and then was gone, moving wraithlike through the night toward Tipi Town.

Andrew Pettigrew, private soldier, sat naked and alone and miserable on the army blanket. He sighed and slowly began dressing.

Ten horses. He made thirteen dollars a month. Of that, over the last three years he had saved exactly one dollar and fifty cents. That gave him fifteen cents apiece to buy ten horses.

There were still wild horses on the plains, but that was no help. Pettigrew stood and buckled his belt. How could he possibly round up ten horses? If he had leave—but he didn't. If he knew how to go about capturing mustangs—but he didn't. If he had more than a buck fifty—Pettigrew snatched up his hat and jammed it angrily onto his head.

Steal them?

A desperate man thinks desperate thoughts, and wanting Dawn Fox as he did, Pettigrew was a desperate man.

Sure, ten horses. Ten army horses. Even a desperate man could see the folly in that. It couldn't be done, first of all. Second, there might be some suspicion after the fact if Pettigrew's father-in-law was seen with ten U.S.-branded bay horses.

Pettigrew stood staring aimlessly toward the encampment where the friendly Indians lived. They stayed near the army installation to avoid being swept up in the hostilities on the plains. And there, in a somewhat decrepit

4

tipi, Dawn Fox would lie down to sleep tonight. Without Pettigrew.

He turned angrily and started stumping off across the broken ground toward the outpost, which appeared as a black, blocky form against the moonlit plains; he was hoping he hadn't been out too long, and that Corson was still on gate guard.

Ten horses.

"Ten cents." Corporal Wojensky, in trousers and boots, long undershirt and galluses, bumped the pot another dime, and Rafferty, grumbling, threw in his hand. Wojensky grinned and glanced at Malone, who had two neat stacks of pennies in front of him.

"Shit." The Irishman looked at his platoon leader again, trying to read his eyes. Cautiously he scooted ten cents toward the untidy pot, called, and spread out three fours.

"Sorry." But Wojensky wasn't a bit sorry. He showed Malone three eights and scraped up his winnings as Malone, his chair screeching angrily against the floor, rose.

"No need to get mad," Wojensky grinned.

"I never get mad," Malone said through gritted teeth.

Reb McBride, the company bugler, laughed loudly from his bunk. Malone's eyes narrowed. He was a brawler and a soldier and a bad drinker. He might have had some knuckles on his meaty fists that weren't broken from fighting, but they weren't evident.

"I got to get on gate watch," Malone said.

"McBride?" Wojensky looked toward the bugler. The game was running out of players with anything in their pockets. It was too close to payday. McBride yawned and waved a hand, refusing.

Malone, stamping into his boots, looked to the corner where Wolfgang Holzer lay reading a book by a man

5

named Goethe. It was an old book, printed in German, which was fortunate for Wolfie, since it was the only language he knew. English seemed to be beyond him. He was a good soldier, but the language barrier was infuriating at times. Malone and others had tried to teach Holzer American, but it just hadn't taken.

"Wolfie! Let's go, we got the duty."

"Oh, *ja*," Holzer said, smiling. He placed his book beneath his pillow and swung his feet to the floor. "We have the watch gate."

"The watch gate?" Reb McBride grinned. "Which one is that."

"The one you tell time by," Rafferty answered.

Holzer, with his limitless good nature, only nodded, smiling. He pulled on his highly polished boots and rose, putting on an unwrinkled shirt. Malone was always amazed at Holzer's ability to remain shaven, pressed, and polished, perhaps because he never quite managed it himself. With his faded shirt rolled up to reveal thick forearms, hat tilted back, cigar clamped in his teeth, Malone was the antithesis of Holzer's military formality. Still, they got along well together; they always had, and on one occasion at least, Holzer had saved Malone's life.

"Now to go for the gate," Holzer said, putting his hat on, picking up his Springfield rifle, which, although as old as anyone else's, looked as if it had been issued yesterday.

"Why'n fuck don't you go home if you can't even learn to speak the goddamn language," a nasal voice said.

Malone and Wojensky turned their heads. McBride sat up. It was Carl Fremont, a new transfer. He was a complainer, a bigot, and an all-around pain in the ass.

Fremont—who claimed to be related to General John Fremont, the explorer, claimed to have a brilliant Civil War record, claimed to be the best marksman ever to

6

come down the pike, the greatest lover and fighter since Adam—was a bulky, middle-aged man, far too old for the stripeless uniform he wore. He talked as though he had a mouthful of sand, he stank, he didn't follow orders. He didn't do a damned bit of work he could slide out from under.

"Go home?" Holzer said, still smiling. He looked toward his bunk. The barracks *was* his home. Holzer had been signed up by an overenthusiastic recruiting officer as he stepped ashore in New York from an immigrant boat. Probably assuming that it was more bureaucratic paperwork, Holzer had signed up, only to find himself in Wyoming three months later, fighting Indians.

"Shut up, Fremont," Malone said.

"I speak my mind."

"I've noticed. Too damned much."

"He a friend of yours?"

"That's right." Malone had taken a step toward Fremont's bunk. Wojensky, smelling trouble, put his cards down and rose. Rafferty, seizing the moment, peeked at the corporal's cards.

"Okay," Wojensky said, "enough of this crap. Malone, get on out to the gate. Holzer . . ." Wojensky tilted his head toward the door and Wolfgang Holzer nodded, striding across the wooden floor toward the door. Rafferty leaned back, smiling.

"Watch yourself," Malone said, pointing a stubby finger at Fremont. Fremont chuckled.

"Sure, Irish." Malone turned and started toward the door, hearing Fremont grumble, "Son of a bitch can't even speak English."

"Raise you fifteen cents," Rafferty said. Wojensky folded, and Rafferty's grin faded.

The stars were bright in an empty sky. The moon, slowly rising, cast long shadows at the base of the stockade wall. Malone glanced toward the captain's quarters, toward the BOQ. Both were dark. There was a light in the company office, where the officer of the day, Mr. Taylor, was on duty, but aside from that lamp, all of Outpost Number Nine was dark. The barracks lamp had been turned out as Malone and Holzer left to relieve Corson and Armstrong.

"Halt! Who goes there?" a voice from the parapet demanded, and Malone snarled, "Your mother, Corson. Who in hell do you think it is?"

"Malone? I didn't think it was that late."

"Time does fly when you're having fun," Malone said, climbing the ladder to the parapet. Holzer would take a turn around the outside of the outpost before joining Malone.

Corson, his coat collar around his ears, came to where Malone waited, staring out at the plains. "No special orders, nothing happening," Corson said.

"Good," Malone replied. "Life's complicated enough as it is."

Corson's voice lowered conspiratorially. "There is one thing."

"Christ," Malone grumbled automatically. "What is it?"

"I let somebody out."

"Without a pass?" Malone looked to the stars.

"Uh...yes."

"Shit."

"It was Pettigrew. You know. The Indian girl."

"You let him out?"

"Uh...yes," Corson said.

"And if you're found out, your ass is in a sling. Now you want me to let him in, and if I do, my ass is beside yours."

"Uh...yeah." Corson grinned and Malone couldn't

8

help smiling in response. He slapped Corson on the shoulder.

"All right. Any man who can find himself a woman around here deserves a little help, I suppose."

"You'll do, Malone," Corson said.

"Yeah. I'll do for a sucker." He looked toward the office where Second Lieutenant Taylor was supposedly awake and alert. "Go on, get out of here," he said to Corson, and Corson, grinning, started down the ladder.

"Shit," Malone breathed.

Holzer had finished his circuit outside the walls and now entered, barring the gate. Malone saw Private Armstrong say something to Holzer, then yawn and straggle off toward the barracks. Malone stood staring at the broad, moon-glossed plains, listening to the distant howl of a coyote, trying not to think too much of other places a man might be on a night like this.

The tapping was so soft that at first Malone didn't hear it. When he did hear it, he wasn't certain that it came from the gate. He peered down over the parapet, saw the blue uniform, and whispered, "Pettigrew?"

There was no answer. Malone heard the gate swing open on iron hinges. At the same moment he saw, from the corner of his eye, the door to the orderly room swing open, painting a brief wedge of yellow across the dark parade. Lieutenant Taylor was crossing toward the gate, making his rounds.

"Wolfie!" Malone hissed, but already the gate had been opened. Already Private Andrew Pettigrew was inside, the gate swinging to. Malone spun around to see Pettigrew scurrying toward the barracks, flitting through the shadows along the wall.

Malone's eyes shuttled to the figure striding across the parade. Had he seen Pettigrew? Malone groaned inwardly. It figured. Corson makes an agreement with Pet-

9

tigrew, and Malone gets tangled up in it. "Only you, you dumb fart," Malone told himself. "Only you. How in hell do you always get caught?"

But he hadn't been, not on this night. Second Lieutenant Taylor came to the gate and spoke to Holzer.

"Everything quiet, Private Holzer?"

"*Ja.*" Wolfie, at rigid attention, saluted. "All so still."

"Who's that up there? Malone?"

"It's me. Mr. Taylor."

"All quiet?"

"Quiet as death, sir."

Taylor nodded. He looked again at Malone, sensing something. Realizing that whatever it was, he would never find out, Taylor saluted them and walked away, continuing his rounds, which included peering into the sutler's store to assure himself no one had been locked in there. Three nights ago, Privates Peabody and Dixon had been locked "accidentally" into Pop Evan's store, supposedly hollering themselves hoarse as they called for help. They hadn't wanted to damage the lock or break a window, they said, and so they continued to holler. All that hollering had dried their voices to a whisper, they had claimed, and at that point it became necessary to break into the three-point-two beer that Pop sold. There hadn't been a hell of a lot left of Peabody and Dixon come morning, so Taylor figured they had also gotten into Pop's stock of illicit whisky.

Tonight everything had been quiet, and that suited Taylor fine. He checked the mess hall door and found it locked; Sergeant Dutch Rothausen, the company cook, insisted that someone had been raiding his larder, but Taylor suspected it was Rothausen's own kitchen help.

Taylor went past the barracks again, just to stretch his legs a little, glanced over to where Holzer and Malone stood their watch, then turned and walked back to the orderly room, where he would read the two-month-old St. Louis newspaper for the third time.

Andrew Pettigrew had just made it. He had been standing in the darkness just inside the enlisted barracks door, his heart pounding as he listened to Mr. Taylor's footsteps approach and then go on by. He hadn't been seen slipping in the gate, thank God.

The last thing Pettigrew wanted, as short as he was, was trouble. Pettigrew stumbled into a chair and someone chuckled.

"Screwed himself blind."

"Shut up," Pettigrew snarled. He made his way to his bunk and sat down.

"Cut that close," Corson said.

"I did for sure," Pettigrew whispered. He unbuttoned his shirt.

"No more of that, Andy. I can't take the risk."

"Corson . . ."

"No more," Corson said flatly.

"But please," a mock falsetto voice that Pettigrew recognized as Carl Fremont's whined, "I have to see my little red baby."

"Shut up, Fremont."

"Everybody shut up," Corporal Wojensky grumbled.

"She slick herself down with bear grease, does she?" Fremont said, ignoring Wojensky.

"Shut up," Fremont said again.

"Don't know how anybody could stand to lay a stinkin' squaw," Fremont said, rolling over.

It was one too many remarks. Andy Pettigrew launched himself across the bunk and hit Fremont's bed, his fist rising and falling, slamming into Fremont's jaw. Fremont rolled out of the sack, kicking free of his blankets to charge at Pettigrew, roaring as he did so.

He hit Pettigrew's midsection with his shoulder and

11

kept going, throwing him to the floor as Pettigrew looped wild blows at his back and shoulders. They slammed to the floor, fists flailing.

"Christ!" McBride muttered. It was getting impossible to sleep here.

"Help me break this up!" Wojensky said, grabbing McBride's arm.

"Not on your life, Corp." McBride covered his head with his blanket.

Wojensky stumbled toward the fighting men, followed by Stretch Dobbs, who had unwound himself from his blankets. Reaching the fighting men, they found Fremont banging Pettigrew's head against the plank floor. Fremont's nose was dripping blood. Fremont had begun yelling, cussing, screaming. If there was a name Pettigrew hadn't called him it was outside of Wojensky's vocabulary.

"Come on, break it up," Wojensky demanded. But they didn't feel inclined to, at this point. Pettigrew shoved the heel of his hand against Fremont's already damaged nose, and the bigger man squealed with pain. Wojensky grabbed Fremont's left arm and Dobbs the right. They dragged him cursing and screaming from Pettigrew. One last wild kick caught Wojensky on the shin, and he hollered with pain.

"See what I mean?" McBride muttered from his bunk.

Wojensky wheeled angrily toward McBride, then swung his attention back to Fremont and Pettigrew. "Dammit, that is all. Unless you want to go on report."

"Indian-lovin' son of a bitch started it," Fremont said, wiping at his nose.

"I don't care who started it!" Wojensky was getting heated up now. "It is ended. Now!"

Pettigrew, still shaking with anger, rose from the floor and walked heavily to his bunk. He lay back, feeling his jaw throb. Loose tooth, he thought. He didn't want to finger it to find out, so he simply lay there in the dark silence, staring at the ceiling as his head hammered away.

He wasn't mad at Fremont anymore. It wasn't worth staying mad at an idiot. Pettigrew had bigger worries just then.

Ten horses.

two ───────────────

Reveille sounded sweet and clear in the dawn stillness. Captain Warner Conway, who was usually up long before the bugler, lingered in bed on this cool morning. He lingered, letting his hand run up the sleek, familiar flank of his wife, Flora.

She was watching him with smiling eyes, loving eyes, those same eyes that had captivated him all those years ago, and still held the spark of that earlier time.

She loved him, would always love him, and he knew it. There are few feelings to compare.

Flora rolled toward him, nestling her head in the hollow of his shoulder, letting her leg rest on his, and he stroked her back gently.

"Time to rise and shine, sir," Flora said.

"That's the sun's duty," the captain answered. He kissed his wife's forehead and swept her hair away from her eyes.

"Why, I thought you were the one who ordered the sun to rise over Outpost Number Nine," Flora said with a teasing smile.

"Yes," he agreed, "one of the commander's many unappreciated duties."

"I appreciate you," she said, rolling onto her back, her smile becoming more than teasing.

"Reveille's sounded," he reminded her.

"You can be too much of a soldier sometimes, Warner," she said.

"Maybe." He considered it seriously for a moment, then, feeling Flora's hand slip to his thigh, he forgot about soldiering and went to her.

She was soft and warm, fragrant in the predawn light, familiar, yet new and intriguing as always. Her thighs were soft against his; her fingers traced patterns across his back.

They made love—sweetly, slowly—and it was, as always, more than a ritual, a need. With Warner and Flora Conway, it had always been an act of love as it was now.

He held her close, feeling the press of her breasts against his chest, feeling the thrust and sway of her hips as she gave of herself, feeling the slow trembling in her thighs, the rush of fluid, the soft residual claspings.

He lay with her and he kissed her. Shoulders, breasts, cheek and ear. She lay back, smiling and content. Finally, Flora slapped his bare ass and said, "Rise and shine, soldier."

"Yes." He sighed. "I'm already late."

"Late? Late for what, Warner? You ought to slow down a little. Sergeant Cohen can handle nearly everything that comes up, and you know it."

"Yes," he answered. It was true; outside of combat decisions, Ben Cohen practically ran the show. But lately something was gnawing at Ben. He seemed distracted.

He wasn't bellowing at the men so much, and that was a bad sign. "There's no trouble between Ben and Maggie, is there?" the captain asked as he rolled from the bed, reaching for his pants.

"Trouble?" Flora Conway yawned expansively and, with a little sigh of determination, got from the bed herself. "Not that I know of. I doubt it, dear. Why do you ask?"

"I don't know. It's nothing, I suppose. Ben just doesn't seem himself lately."

"I'm sure it's nothing to worry about."

"No, probably not."

Flora was slicing bread, but Conway, putting his arms around her waist, told her, "I don't want to eat this morning."

"You're sure?"

"Positive. I'll have coffee at the office. That's all."

"You don't have to go," she said, turning to wrap her arms around his neck. "Not really."

"Really," he answered. He kissed her lightly and went to finish dressing. Ten minutes later, shaved and shined, Captain Warner Conway went out onto the plankwalk before his quarters to survey his domain. Outpost Number Nine, a bleak, officially ignored installation on the Wyoming plains. A place visitors hastened away from, residents despised. It had seen some high drama and some tragedy, but it hadn't taken on character. It remained dreary, businesslike, unremarkable.

"Morning, sir," Lieutenant Kincaid said, snapping Conway a salute.

"Morning, Matt. Everything quiet, I hope?"

"As far as I know. Haven't seen a hostile all morning. None in the mess hall."

Conway smiled thinly as they turned and walked together toward the captain's office. The men were emerging in small groups from the mess, forming up slowly as Sergeant Gus Olsen waited, hands on hips.

"Just patrol toward the foothills, Matt," Conway said. "Shell Eye is probably still in the area, although no one's seen him. You might swing by the agency and see if any of the friendlies have spotted him."

"Shall I take Windy?"

"Not unless you really think you need him. He's only had a day's rest in the last month."

"We'll make do," Kincaid replied, although he would have preferred to have the civilian scout with him. The fellow was crusty and mostly silent, but he knew his job. He looked Indian, but denied it vehemently. He claimed to be Armenian, and maybe he was. No one knew a lot about Windy Mandalian, except that he had been here as long as the buffalo, and would probably still be here when the last of the buffalo were gone.

Matt left the captain at the orderly room door, and crossed the parade toward Gus Olsen, who was forming up the patrol. Other soldiers studied the duty roster or lounged near the mess hall, spurring themselves into motion as they spied the approaching officer.

Conway went into the orderly room, nodding good morning to the company clerk. Ben Cohen, like a great, uniformed grizzly bear, sat sagging behind his desk. He rose to his feet as Conway entered.

"Coffee's on, sir," Cohen said.

"Very well. Anything hot going on?"

"I'm not sure how hot it is, sir, but there's a dispatch from Regiment on your desk. Also a private soldier waiting to see you." Ben nodded toward the corner chair, and for the first time Conway was aware of Private Andrew Pettigrew's presence.

17

"Good morning, Private." Pettigrew came to his feet. He had, Conway noticed, a beautiful shiner decorating his right eye.

"Good morning, sir," Pettigrew responded nervously.

"Was there something you needed?" the captain asked.

Pettigrew glanced at Ben Cohen and at the clerk. "It's in the nature of a private matter, sir," Pettigrew said.

"Very well, come into my office."

Pettigrew followed the captain in and hesitantly took the seat the captain offered him.

"What is it, then?" Conway asked, noticing the dispatch from Regiment on his desk.

"Well, sir, I guess by the manual I'm supposed to talk to you." Pettigrew swallowed dryly and fought on. "It's about me, sir. There's a girl, you see. I might want to get married," he blurted out.

"You *might*?" Conway frowned and rose to sit on the corner of his desk, facing Pettigrew. "If you're not sure, Pettigrew, I'd certainly advise you to wait. Where in the world did you meet a woman out here?"

"I met her—she lives here," Pettigrew said. "But it's not that I'm not sure I want to get married, sir. It's that I'm not sure I *can*."

"Would you like a cup of coffee?" Conway asked. "No? I'll have one."

Shaking his head, Conway went out into the orderly room, where Cohen was moping over his dailies. He poured himself a cup of coffee, hoping Pettigrew would organize his thoughts in his absence.

"Well?" Conway said on his return. "Why don't you lay it all out for me, Pettigrew?"

"I'll try, sir." Pettigrew's shoulders lifted in a massive sigh. "You see, the girl I want to marry—well, she's Sioux. She lives in Tipi Town."

"You're not sure you want to marry an Indian?"

18

"No, sir. I'm not not sure because she's an Indian."

Conway was sorry he had asked. "It's a difficult situation, Pettigrew," he said.

"Yes, sir, I realize that. But I wasn't planning on going back East, where folks mightn't understand. We mean to live out here, where it ain't that unusual. Thing is, I kind of got myself into a bind. I mean, I want to marry Dawn Fox right away, but I ain't sure I can wangle it. So I might not be getting married until after I'm discharged. But the thing is, I might, so I wanted to tell you."

Conway didn't try to interpret that. He let Pettigrew go on. "You see, her father, Big Nose, he won't let Dawn Fox marry me unless and until I can come up with the marriage price—which is the way they do these things," he explained unnecessarily. "That is, he wants ten horses before he'll let me marry his daughter. Well, I don't have ten horses and I don't have the money to buy ten horses, so I likely will have to wait until I'm discharged and go off horse-hunting. Unless Black Hatchet moves in meanwhile."

"Black Hatchet? Oh, you have a rival."

"That's it, sir, and he's got ten ponies. So I don't really know how I'm going to do this, but I'm going to get married as soon as I can, and I wanted to tell you."

"Yes." Conway blinked twice and rose. "I'm glad you came to me, Pettigrew. When things get more settled, you will let me know."

"Yes, sir. I surely will. Just wish I had them ten horses."

Conway showed him to the door and refilled his coffee cup. Windy Mandalian had come in while Conway was closeted with Pettigrew, and the captain nodded to the scout.

"Coffee, Windy?"

19

"I'm about full up, sir," Mandalian said, lifting his lanky, buckskin-clad frame from the chair. "Just stopped by to see what the situation was. I seen Matt Kincaid going out on patrol, so I figured I was off duty."

"You are. Come on into my office."

Windy accepted. He glanced at Cohen on the way by, and then looked questioningly at the captain. Cohen looked like a sack of skin encased in a blue shirt. Conway shook his head in response to Windy's unspoken question.

"He sick or somethin'?" Windy asked, once they were in Conway's office.

"He says he's not." Conway reached into his bottom desk drawer and removed the whiskey bottle, passing it to Windy, who smiled and poured a dollop in his coffee cup.

"Likely he's getting cabin fever," Windy suggested after taking a sip of the whiskey and nodding appreciatively. "Ben's needed at that desk, I reckon, but he *is* a soldier. When was the last time he was in the field?"

Conway couldn't even recall. He turned Windy's thought over in his mind. It was possible. That stale feeling Conway himself got once in a while could be what was afflicting Ben. A soldier like Cohen would never mention feeling bogged down, locked up. Conway shoved the thought to the back of his mind.

The captain told Windy about Andy Pettigrew. Mandalian listened thoughtfully. "I heard something about that down in Tipi Town. Sometimes them marriages don't work out half bad, Captain. Not if the man don't expect to take a Sioux and make her into a white woman."

"Talking to Pettigrew, I didn't get the idea that he wanted to do anything like that. He wants to settle out here somewhere."

"Then it might work. I suppose the boy's got as good

20

a chance as anyone of being happy. But I do know he's got one problem he'll have to solve."

"Black Hatchet?"

"Absolutely," Windy nodded. "I know that young buck, and he's trouble. If he wants Dawn Fox for his wife, he'll try to have her, whatever it takes."

"That's no good," Conway said. They didn't need an incident with the friendly Indians, but short of forbidding Pettigrew to visit the girl—something that was, strictly speaking, outside of Conway's powers—there wasn't much to be done.

Windy rose. "If I'm off duty, sir, I believe I'll amble over to Pop's, pick up a few things, and go on down home." Home being, for Mandalian, a tipi he shared with an energetic, handsome Indian woman who may or may not have been his wife.

Conway bade the scout farewell and then turned to the business of the day. He picked up the communique from Regiment, read it, cursed softly, read it again, and cursed a little more loudly.

"Son of a bitch!" he finally bellowed.

"Sir?" Second Lieutenant Fitzgerald stood in the captain's doorway, grinning.

"Not you, Fitz, come in." Conway waved a weary hand. He reached for his desk drawer handle. "When Windy was here, I thought it was too early for a drink. But now," he said as he plopped the bottle on his desk and reached for his mug, "it definitely is not."

"What is it?" a puzzled Fitzgerald asked. Conway shoved the message from Regiment over to his junior officer.

"Why us?" Conway grumbled, tilting the bottle to splash some bourbon into his coffee.

Fitzgerald was reading the communique.

To: Captain Warner Conway, Commanding,
Outpost Number Nine, Wyoming Territory

Dear Captain Conway:

Be advised that on or about June 30, Lord Alvin
Whitechapel, Earl of Lynley, and members of his
family and retinue, will arrive at Outpost Number
Nine. The purposes of the visit are exploration of
the frontier, and hunting. It is essential that Lord
Whitechapel and all members of his entourage be
extended every courtesy and given utmost coop-
eration.

Yours truly,
Lt. Col. John Pembroke, U.S.A.
(Via State Dept., via War Dept.)

Fitzgerald was frowning as deeply as the captain now.
He handed the communique back. "The colonel has a
way with understatement, doesn't he? 'Via State Department, via War.' The noble lord seems to carry some
weight."

"Yes," Conway sighed, "so it seems. We don't really
need this, do we, Fitz? A party of Englishmen looking
for trophies and souvenirs of the Wild West. And I get
the idea," he said, scanning the letter again, "that any
recommendations I make had better be in the form of a
request."

"We haven't had a lot of hostile activity," Fitz said
hopefully.

"Shell Eye is back."

"We've got until the thirtieth," Fitzgerald said. "Plenty
of time for cleanup and preparations. How much trouble
can a handful of Englishmen be?"

Conway had to admit that there wasn't much to be

done about it, except for a little cleaning up. They had no red carpet to roll out and no ox to roast. Perhaps it would all work out well enough.

Andy Pettigrew was sure nothing would ever work out well again in his life. He and Private Malone were behind the outpost, digging a new latrine pit. A necessary job, but a tough one, especially at this time of year, when the rains were long gone, when the sun had baked the prairie earth to the consistency of brick.

"What'd you do?" Malone asked, leaning on his pick.

"What?" Pettigrew's eyes returned from vast distances to focus on Malone.

"How'd you draw this detail?" Malone said.

Pettigrew shrugged, "My name was on the list."

Malone saw he wasn't going to get much information from Pettigrew. The man was getting hard to talk to. Malone had been trying to figure out just how he himself had gotten on Ben Cohen's shit list, and he thought that by finding out what Pettigrew had done, he might come to an understanding of what he himself was being punished for.

This *had* to be a punishment detail. Malone wiped the sweat from his eyes with the back of his hand and squinted into the white sky. He sighed and began chipping at the earth with his pick.

"What the hell did I do?" he wondered. Three nights back he had been a little bit drunk and he found he didn't have a good recollection of all the events of that somewhat blurry evening, but he couldn't recall doing anything that Cohen could have found out about.

Malone, grumbling, his shoulder and back muscles working easily, bent to his task. The pick rose and fell, hardly biting into the hard clay earth. Pettigrew worked absently, his eyes somewhere distant, his mind on another plane. Malone tried a little more conversation, but it went nowhere.

Another half hour of that, and Malone had to call a halt. He tossed the pick aside and snatched up the canteen, pouring a little of the tepid water over his head before putting his hat back on.

It was then that he noticed the other man.

"Who the hell's that?" Malone asked.

Pettigrew straightened up and turned, wiping his own brow. There he was, sitting a paint pony: a strong-looking young Sioux brave, a repeating rifle cradled in his arm. He simply sat staring at Pettigrew as the wind shifted the feathers knotted into his hair. It was Black Hatchet.

"I don't know," Pettigrew lied.

"Get out of here!"Malone shouted at the Indian. "I don't fancy having an armed Indian sitting watch over me," he said in a lower voice.

Black Hatchet didn't move. He might have been a statue erected to the Noble Savage. "Get out of here!" Malone shouted again. Pettigrew went silently back to work. Grumbling, Malone did the same.

He glanced from time to time at Black Hatchet, having no idea at all what notion had prompted this particular Indian to sit and watch them dig a latrine pit. He was simply there—and then he wasn't.

Malone straightened up, scratching his head. He looked around, but failed to locate the Sioux. That was surely a soft-footed horse.

"Crazy bastard," he muttered. "Don't know what in hell's going on in their minds, sometimes."

Malone didn't, but Pettigrew did, and he didn't like it one bit.

three ──────────────

The arrival was heralded by a dust cloud over the plains, an awed curse from the gate guard, and a hastily delivered message to the commanding officer. "They're coming!" Private Armstrong said, banging open the orderly room door. Ben Cohen flared up.

"Is that the way you report now, Armstrong? Goddammit, *who's* coming?"

"The civilians. Sergeant, you never seen anything like this."

"I've seen plenty of civilians," Cohen said. He rose and straightened the uncomfortable dress tunic he had been wearing for a week in anticipation of this moment. Then, rapping on the captain's door, he went in.

"They're coming, sir. Gate guard's spotted them."

"Very well."

"Honor guard?" Cohen asked.

"No, let's keep something in reserve," Conway said

dryly. "If Lord Whitechapel wants a parade, we'll give it to him. For now, let's just try to look sharp. I'll find out what kind of man he is, and we'll go from there."

At the gate, Armstrong and Wheeler stood in awed silence. They watched the long caravan approaching from the south, led by an enclosed wagon with gold scrollwork and a dozen outriders. Behind the wagon came six ox-drawn Conestogas, more outriders, a dozen or so horse-drawn carts, then more outriders. Behind them was the horse herd, easily a hundred animals being driven by men and dogs. The duke's retinue was easily the size of a small wagon train.

"Must be forty men," Wheeler said. "What in hell are they for?"

Armstrong had no idea. He counted himself a hunter, but he had never seen anything like this: an army of men crossing the plains in the pursuit of game.

Captain Conway himself had walked to the gate, and he was no less stunned than were his men. He had heard of these great English sportsmen and their great appetites, but somehow he hadn't expected this. Not at Outpost Number Nine, not in Wyoming.

The titled families of Europe had long eagerly pursued the "blood sports," and the great safaris in Africa and India were legend. These men had the financial resources to provide themselves with creature comforts, even luxuries, no matter where the hunt took them. Often such a caravan bore all the appurtenances necessary to surround His Lordship with the conveniences he would enjoy if he'd never left his ancestral estate.

"What have we, sir?" Fitzgerald asked.

Conway glanced at his lieutenant. "God knows, Mr. Fitzgerald."

Fitzgerald, squinting into the sun, was now gaping.

Conway glanced back at the parade. "We don't even

26

have room for all His Lordship's gear. Look at the horses—must be a hundred of them. A treasure trove for the hostiles, assuming they have the nerve to attack a party as large as this one. Make ready, Mr. Fitzgerald. It appears our English cousins have arrived."

Conway wished suddenly that he had formed an honor guard, but it was too late for second thoughts. The lead wagon was nearly to the main gate. Sergeant Cohen appeared at the captain's side.

"They're not all going to try to cram in here, are they?" he asked no one in particular.

The dust cloud behind the caravan was immense, stretching high into the blue skies of Wyoming. Dozens of Indians had appeared from Tipi Town, and they now sat their horses or raced along beside the caravan, enjoying the parade.

The lead wagon, driven by a man in red livery, rolled in through the gate. A mustached man in a blue uniform, much embellished with gold braid sat beside the driver. Neither one looked right or left as they rolled onto parade.

Behind them came the earl himself.

It had to be him, Conway knew at first glance. Tall, silver-mustached, erect. He had hooded eyes and an ambitious nose, and was dressed in twill trousers, a suede jacket, and an enormous white pith helmet.

The magnificent black horse he rode sidestepped past the captain, tossing its head.

It looked as if the rest of the party did indeed intend to follow Lord Whitechapel blindly into the outpost. The caravan continued to roll forward, creaking, squealing, barking, clomping, thundering.

"Hold them up, Ben," Captain Conway said. "Have them circle up. They'll want to water their stock at the creek. I'll explain it to—"

An ox-drawn wagon had already entered the outpost,

27

rolling past Conway behind a wall of dust, and the captain turned away, closing his eyes.

"Ben!"

"I'm gone, sir." Seconds later, Ben's voice was raised into a bull roar as he shouted at the drivers and horsemen.

"Sir!" A strange, high-pitched voice carried across the parade. "Commander of this post! Where are you, sir!"

Conway turned to see Whitechapel in front of the office, bellowing for him. Swallowing a curse, Conway turned and strode rapidly toward the nobleman, noting with dismay that his own uniform was now coated with dust.

He caught a glimpse of Flora, in her best blue dress, peering out of the window of their quarters. Glancing back, he saw Cohen, pursued by a yapping long-haired dog, heading off the influx.

"Sir? Lord Whitechapel? I am Captain Conway, commanding officer of this outpost."

Whitechapel looked around and nodded. He was obviously looking for someone to hold his horse while he dismounted, and Conway obliged.

"I'll take him, sir." Fitzgerald relieved Conway of the black charger, and Conway was left alone with Lord Alvin Whitechapel, a taller man than Conway had thought, militarily erect, a hint of amusement dancing in his pale gray eyes.

"Shall we go into my office?" Conway asked.

"Nothing would please me more, Captain. Damned sorry to raise such a row."

"It's nothing at all. Please, step in."

They passed through the orderly room, Whitechapel looking appraisingly at the map on the wall, the regimental colors, the old saber.

"Please, sir, sit down."

"I've been seated all morning, Captain," Whitechapel

said. There was no smile on that broad mouth, but the eyes twinkled more furiously.

"Then, sir, may I offer you a drink?"

"You may, and I accept gratefully," Whitechapel said.

Conway was wishing he had thought to bring the bonded whiskey to his office, but Whitechapel seemed unconcerned. He accepted the whiskey from Conway, and stood rocking on the balls of his feet, sipping it.

"As I say, sorry to raise such a fuss. I know it's a bit rugged out on the frontier. All you need is some rambling gamesman clogging things up, eh?"

"Not at all," Conway replied.

"Well, we won't trouble you much, sir, you have my word on that. We'll need a few men to assist in the camp labor, of course."

"Of course," Conway said automatically. Didn't the man already have thirty camp laborers out there?

"And a scout would be helpful. I have my own man out getting the lay of the land right now, of course, but familiarity does help. You have someone?"

"I can provide someone," Conway assured the earl. Who? Damned if he was going to loan Windy out!

"That's settled, then." Whitechapel finished the whiskey and placed the glass on the captain's desk. "We'll bivouac here for a few days, get the arms prepared, rest the stock, then we'll be ready to embark."

"Fine." Conway asked, "How long will you be with us, sir, in Wyoming?"

"Can't say at the moment, Conway. Through the summer, I should imagine. Possibly through the winter, and depart in the spring if the weather turns too nasty for decent traveling."

Conway couldn't have spoken, even if an answer had occurred to him. Through the summer, possibly through the winter! Good God, month after month of these people

29

wandering the plains, merrily shooting off guns, while the hostiles gather and watch, tempted by the obvious wealth of the party!

"Hope we're not putting you out," Whitechapel said.

"No, not at all."

"Well then, I'm sure it will all be quite marvelous. We'll try to stay out of the military's way, old man. I know how it is. I was in India during the Sepoy Mutiny. Did a bit of soldiering myself. More to combat boredom than from any real calling, I must admit. Different with you career chaps, I should imagine."

"Perhaps."

"Well then, happy to have spoken with you." Whitechapel's hand was thrust out, and Conway shook it, finding the hand dry and strong. "We'll expect you and your officers and your ladies for tea. I expect Farnsworth has already gotten half the camp set up. An excellent camp manager. Well, later, then. Good morning, sir."

The nobleman was out the door before Conway could come around his desk and escort him. The captain stood there for a moment, staring at the empty doorway, then he sank into his chair, pouring more than the usual dollop into his whiskey glass.

"Sir?" Fitzgerald was in the doorway. "Any special orders? They're setting up camp a quarter-mile downstream. All very efficient and neat."

"No orders." Conway looked at Fitzgerald and asked soberly, "What time do the English have their tea?"

He didn't find out until he had asked Flora, who told him, "Why, at four, dear, and we're invited? How charming, but why didn't you ask Lord Whitechapel to dine with us? I'm sure it would have been much nicer for him than having to take his meal in a tent."

"Didn't think of it, to tell you the truth. Didn't have time to think of it." Conway was trying to put the luster back on his boots. He sat on the edge of the settee, watching Flora, who was arranging and rearranging her hair.

"Is he . . . well, what is he like, Warner? Not one of those awful snobs we hear about?"

"I don't think so. He didn't strike me that way, and I suppose that if he were, we wouldn't have gotten an invitation to tea. No." Conway dabbed at his boot with polish. "He's arrogant without being haughty—privileges of class and all, you know—intelligent and, I believe, witty, although that's just an impression. We weren't together that long. It was simply a matter of his telling me what he was going to do, while I mutely bobbed my head like any good servant."

"You make him sound awful!" Flora laughed.

"Do I? I don't think he is awful, actually. It's just that he's always had his own way, and any other hasn't even occurred to him. I don't imagine he's unique in that respect among his peers. Still, it doesn't go down well over here, does it?"

Glancing at his watch, Captain Conway got up and walked to his wife, kissing her lightly on the cheek. He held her at arm's length for a minute, just smiling at her.

"What?" she asked.

"I just wanted a look to get me through the afternoon."

"You're turning into a regular romantic in your old age," Flora laughed. "You'll be coming home early?"

"Yes, sometime after three. I'll want a fresh shave, then we'll walk on over and see how the peerage manages in our wild West."

Outside, the sun was a hard glare. Downriver, Conway could see half a dozen tents set up, one of them a huge thing perhaps fifty feet long. He heard a cry go up from the gate and walked that way, halting as he saw the column of soldiers, Kincaid at their head, riding in.

31

Conway walked to the office, saw Ben Cohen sitting with a blank expression behind his desk, and said, "Lieutenant Kincaid will be over in a few minutes, Sergeant. Send him right in."

"Yes, sir."

Conway looked again at Ben, frowned, and went into his office to stand before his wall map, lost in thought. It was fifteen minutes before Matt Kincaid arrived.

"Anything, Matt?"

"Not much, sir. We found a few old tracks, which may or may not have been Shell Eye's. The friendlies down at the agency knew nothing, or admitted nothing. I saw our new tent town out there. Lord Whitechapel?"

"That's right. We're invited to tea this afternoon. All of us. I expect you'd better get cleaned up."

Kincaid's mouth twitched slightly. That was all he needed after a long patrol, tea with His Lordship. "Yes, sir," he muttered unhappily.

"I think, Matt, I'm going to put you on something you won't like very much at all." Kincaid's eyebrows lifted.

"Sir?"

"His Lordship needs a guide."

"Yes, sir." Kincaid's face reflected a complete and understandable lack of enthusiasm.

"I'm sending Cohen along."

"The first shirt? I know this Englishman has pull, sir, but can you spare Ben Cohen?"

"I'm doing this for Ben's sake, Matt." Conway sat behind his desk. "He needs a change in duty, I think. You'll have to pick up a half-dozen other men; they'll be laborers and an informal escort. If there's a chance Shell Eye's around, we'd be remiss if we didn't provide some sort of protection. I doubt most of Lord White-

chapel's men have seen any sort of action, the Sepoy
Mutiny aside."

"Sir?" Kincaid frowned in puzzlement.

"Nothing," Conway sighed, "nothing at all."

"Well?" Mr. Taylor looked around at Matt Kincaid from
the mirror in the bachelor officers' quarters.

"You look sharp," Kincaid told him.

"Wish to hell I was out chasing Shell Eye," Taylor
muttered.

"Instead of having tea with His Lordship?" Kincaid's
mock astonishment didn't draw a smile from Taylor, who
adjusted his seldom-worn saber and stepped back from
the mirror again.

"At least," Matt said, "you don't have to spend the
best part of the summer with the man."

Taylor seemed to brighten a little. "That's true. I
always thought the captain kind of favored you, Matt.
What did you do wrong?"

"No idea," Matt said with a grin. "Want to take my
place?"

"Not on your life. I'm only hoping I can escape with
this one obligation satisfied."

"Not a social climber, are you?"

"Not exactly."

The door opened, and Lieutenant Fitzgerald tramped
in. Suppressing a smile, he looked at Matt and then at
Taylor.

"But Mr. Fitzgerald obviously is," Taylor said.

"Is what?" Fitzgerald crossed the room to brush his
hair before the mirror Taylor had abandoned.

"A social climber. Matt wants someone to relieve him
of his obligations."

"No, thanks!" Fitzgerald turned and spread his arms,

33

displaying his splendor. "One afternoon of this is enough. I'm not cut out for politicking. I think the captain made a wise decision in assigning Lieutenant Kincaid to the noble lord."

Kincaid had just opened his mouth to protest when the knock sounded on the BOQ door. Captain Conway and his lady stood there.

"Ready, gentlemen?" the captain asked, and since the question was actually an order, none of them gave the answer that was on their minds.

four ──────────────────

Flora Conway held her husband's arm as they walked beneath the red-and-green-striped canopy toward the tent where Lord Whitechapel was to serve their tea. She whispered to Warner, "And I scolded you for not inviting him to our quarters!"

She had believed that the Earl of Lynley would be more comfortable in her living room than in some canvas camp tent, but she had had no idea that Lord Whitechapel's camp tent would be some fifty feet long by thirty wide, decorated with his colors, festooned with tassels. Nor could she possibly have expected what they would find inside.

They were met at the entrance to the tent by a footman in a clawhammer coat and white shirt. He bowed stiffly, and led the party into the interior of the tent. Flora and Warner Conway led the way, followed by the junior officers.

Flora gasped helplessly. A long table set with linen, crystal, and silver occupied the center of the tent. On the walls of the tent hung the royal colors, African zebra-skin shields, and bright pennants emblazoned with gold lions. Lord Whitechapel sat at the head of the table and he rose now, crossing the Turkish carpets that were spread across the wooden floor.

He wore a green velvet smoking jacket, highly polished boots with silver buckles, and Scotch tweed trousers. Without irony, he apologized.

"One must expect to rough it a little, but we have tried to provide ourselves with a few creature comforts. Enough, one hopes, to avoid embarrassment when entertaining."

There wasn't much danger of that, Conway decided. The candelabra on the table were lit by the footman, and Whitechapel resumed his seat at the head of the table as Conway held Flora's chair and Fitzgerald, Taylor, and Kincaid seated themselves uneasily in the padded leather chairs.

A silent, white-coated servant appeared. Walking to the head of the table, he upturned a crystal goblet, pouring an ounce of red wine for the earl to taste. He did so, nodded dry approval, and allowed the servant to fill his glass.

"A subdued little burgundy," Whitechapel said. "I hope it proves acceptable."

Conway, who had somehow expected only a pot of tea and perhaps some biscuits, tasted his wine, found it excellent, and complimented his host.

"What can be keeping them?" Whitechapel said aloud. He glanced around and almost immediately was rewarded with the expected arrivals. "Ah," he said, standing, "I see the extra time spent at your toilet has yielded divine results."

36

He was beaming with pleasure, and he should have been. Whitechapel took the woman's hand and said, "Gentlemen, may I introduce my wife?"

Conway stood. Matt Kincaid sat gaping. Taylor nearly spilled his wine.

Lady Virginia Whitechapel was a good thirty years younger than her husband, a striking honey blonde with even features, a small nose, full lips, deep green eyes, and a figure of the sort seldom seen outside a sculptor's imagination.

She was seated at the foot of the table, and introductions were made all around. "Good afternoon," was all she said, and that was in an extremely languid, terribly bored tone of voice.

Flora ventured a remark on Her Ladyship's hair, which was intricately done, a strand of pearls weaving its artistic way through the pale curls. All Flora received for an answer was a weary smile.

Serving maids were filling the table with silver platters piled high with delicacies: Comice pears preserved in creme de menthe, chicken breasts in aspic, a chocolate cake hung with white frosting bunting, a tray of mixed nuts, Chinese figs, Turkish delight, and smoked, slivered pork garnished with almonds.

The earl was more interested in the champagne, which was delivered to the head of the table by a patient servant with a wisp of white hair pasted to his skull.

His Lordship sipped it and frowned. Not chilled enough, apparently, the only method of chilling available being to immerse the bottle in the cool stream that ran beside the camp.

Lord Whitechapel gestured distastefully, and the servant hastily removed the champagne.

"Will all of these young officers be escorting us, Captain Conway?" Lord Whitechapel asked.

"No, sir. Just Lieutenant Kincaid here."

"Oh, yes, can't disrupt the entire Western army, can we?" Whitechapel seemed to find his own remark amusing. He chuckled softly. Maybe it was the burgundy.

"What exactly are your intentions, sir?" Conway asked. "I have been given only the vaguest idea of your aims."

"My aims? Record heads, sir."

"Elk?"

"Elk, yes, sir. Elk and buffalo. Deer, antelope, grizzly. Mountain panther."

"I'm afraid you won't find bear or cougar close around here."

"No, I realize that," Whitechapel said. "We'll have to work toward the Medicine Bows, I suppose. See a bit of country, eh, Lieutenant Kincaid? Know that area, do you?"

"Well enough, sir," Kincaid responded. Kincaid shifted uneasily. It was not the clouded gaze of Whitechapel that bothered him. It was the woman.

She sat there cool and elegant, the candlelight sparkling in her eyes, dancing across the jewels at her breast, as she sipped wine from a crystal glass, her eyes above the rim of the cup fixed on Matt Kincaid.

"My husband takes . . . trophies," Lady Whitechapel said, still looking intently at the uncomfortable Matt Kincaid. "It's a sort of silly competition between him and Lord Bertram."

"Virginia!" Whitechapel scolded boisterously. "You speak as though it were all foolishness. It isn't. Lord Bertram has been trying to outdo me for years. Infantile competition. I brought back a fourteen-foot Bengal tiger, and nothing would do but for Lord Bertram immediately to set out for India. He took eighteen months at it, but he returned finally with a larger tiger. He crowed for months over that."

"I see," Conway murmured, placing his hand over his glass as the silent servant tried to fill it with more burgundy. Taylor was silent, his mouth opening only to admit more of the delicacies Lord Whitechapel served at tea. It was a good thing Taylor wasn't going on this expedition, Conway thought; he'd return as fat as a hog.

Flora sat biting daintily at a piece of chocolate cake served by one of the uniformed girls. Her ear had not failed to detect the peculiar emphasis Lady Whitechapel had placed on the word *trophy*, as she looked at Matt Kincaid, and Flora decided that Matt was in for an interesting time.

"Damned mummy topped me," Whitechapel said loudly. Heads came around to stare in puzzlement at his Lordship.

"Lord Bertram," Virginia Whitechapel put in.

"Fellow donated a mummy and a sarcophagus to the Rutledge."

"Rutledge Museum," Lady Whitechapel clarified. "My husband and Lord Bertram have been rivals in the area of cultural artifacts for many years."

"Started in the fifties," Whitechapel said. "Found a striking group of marbles in Siam. Not supposed to be much marble sculpture in that part of the world. Brought it home and gave it to the curator at the Rutledge—made a damned fine display."

"And the following season Lord Bertram went to Africa and brought back hundreds of examples of native art," his wife said.

"They made a fuss over that. Couldn't match the Siamese marbles in my view, but down at the Rutledge they got fairly excited about it, damn Bertram's eyes."

Conway made what he hoped were sympathetic noises and glanced at his men. Taylor and Fitzgerald had cleared away most of the food before them and now were relax-

39

ing, overstuffed, sipping at their wine. Taylor appeared a little glazed over.

Matt Kincaid was a different story. He hadn't eaten much, and he now sat erect in his leather chair, with an electric alertness flashing in his eyes. Conway was momentarily puzzled—until he happened to glance at Lady Whitechapel.

She sat, chin resting on her folded hands, eyes soft and dreamy. Very bored, very feline, very dangerous. Whitechapel himself was looking that way, and Conway leaped in with both feet. "When will you be wanting to pull out, sir?"

"Eh?" Whitechapel's attention was diverted to the captain. "Three days, I expect. Yes, Wednesday, is it? Well"—he frowned thoughtfully—"make it Friday morning. Sunup."

"Fine. If you need anything, of course, don't hesitate to send someone over to the outpost." Conway rose, his officers following suit. "For now, I'm afraid we have our duties."

"Yes, of course. I quite understand." Lord Whitechapel rose as well. "Been a military man myself. Would you care to dine with us this evening, Captain Conway? You and your charming wife? I hardly had a chance to speak to her. Give us a chance to put on the dog a little bit, if you'd care to join us."

"There is nothing I would enjoy more, sir," Conway replied. "Unfortunately, I must decline. I have pressing business back at the outpost." Conway caught a cool glance from Flora. "Otherwise . . ."

"Of course, of course. Shame. Rest of the party wasn't here for tea. Where did Suzanne and Benjamin get off to, Virginia? Well, no matter. Good day, sir," he said, walking to the door with Conway. "Good day."

Virginia Whitechapel remained seated, her smile enigmatic and slight. Conway shook hands with the earl and left the tent, breathing a sigh of relief. He wanted only to get home and pull his boots off.

"We could have dined with them, dear," Flora said.

"Yes. It would have been interesting. With what they serve for tea, I wonder what dinner would be like. Roast boar, seven wines? My God, how can anyone travel the plains like that?"

"I suppose Lord Whitechapel couldn't travel any other way."

"I suppose not."

Behind the captain, Fitzgerald was muttering to Kincaid. "Tough assignment, Matt. Knew there was something to the privilege of rank."

"What are you talking about?" Matt asked with some irritation.

"God, man, do you think I'm blind? That woman was positively leering at you."

"Charm," Kincaid told the second lieutenant. "The lady recognizes a truly masculine man when she sees one."

"Husband's sixty years old if he's a day. How old's she? Twenty?"

"No need to start growling about it, Fitz."

"Growling? Matt, I'm crying."

Captain Conway left his wife at the orderly room door and went in to find Ben Cohen closing up his desk for the day. The duty corporal, Corporal Miller, was there; Four Eyes Bradshaw had already gone.

"Nothing stirring, Ben?"

"Nothing, sir."

"Good." Conway hesitated "Ben, how'd you like to get out of the office for a while?"

"Sir?" Cohen cocked his bull-like head.

41

"I have an assignment for you, and it's one that will require you to be in the field for a time. Of course, if you don't want the job . . ."

"May I ask what it is before deciding, sir?"

"I want you to go along with His Lordship. I'm sending Matt, of course, but he'll have six enlisted men with him, and I'd like someone to supervise. Besides, they're heading for the Medicine Bow foothills, and you know that area better than Matt does."

"I wouldn't say that, sir," Cohen objected. All the same, he seemed to be brightening, puffing up a little.

"Of course, you may not want to leave Maggie for an extended period."

Cohen shook his head. "Truth is, sir, I think maybe Maggie would be happy to see me out of the house for a while. I've been kind of . . . a little out of sorts, sir."

"Oh?" Conway tried to act surprised at this revelation. "Well, absence makes the heart grow fonder."

"Yes, sir. I'd be happy to go along, sir—that is, if you can spare me."

"We'll make do, Ben."

Ben Cohen seemed to grow larger each moment. He was glowing with excitement. Conway was glad he had made this decision. Thinking about it, Conway was damned if he wouldn't like to go himself. "I can guarantee the food," the captain said.

"Yes, sir. How is he, Captain? Lord Whitechapel, that is?"

"You'll like him, Ben. He's not like us, but he's decent. That's my judgment on short acquaintance, anyway."

"Well, sir, I'll get along home then, start making ready."

"He's not pulling out until Friday, Ben."

"I know, sir, I know," Cohen said with a broad wink, "but I figure it's time to start saying goodbye to Maggie."

The detail list was posted at six o'clock by Lieutenant Kincaid. He simply posted it in the barracks, since all the men were out of Wojensky's squad, Wilson's squad having just returned from patrol, Miller's being scheduled out after Shell Eye in the morning.

The invariable griping echoed through the barracks.

"Why me?" Malone anguished. "Christ, why always me?"

"That's soft duty, Malone," Stretch Dobbs calculated. "God, beats a dozen jobs I can think of."

"You'll notice they're not leaving till Friday. That gives me time to finish that latrine pit," Malone grumbled.

"He'll have to kiss his beer goodbye," Carl Fremont said.

"I'd like to kiss *you* goodbye, Fremont." No such luck. Fremont was on the list as well.

So was Pettigrew, and he was wailing, "I can't go, for God's sake! I've only got two months left. What if we don't make it back?"

"What if that Sioux buck makes off with your squaw, you mean," Fremont said, laughing indecently.

Scowling, Andy Pettigrew sagged onto his bunk. It was true. Carl Fremont was exactly right. If he was out roaming the plains with this Englishman for two months, there was every chance that Black Hatchet and Dawn Fox would be married by the time he returned.

Holzer was beaming. "Going to trek with the English rascals!" he slapped Malone on the back. " Cheers! Great English rascals."

"Cheers," Malone muttered.

Rafferty and Corson rounded out the roster. Both of them figured it for soft duty and they were pleased with the assignment. At least it was something different. It beat scavenging for buffalo chips, and it surely beat fighting a hostile for your scalp.

"Who's in charge of this outfit, Wojensky?" Malone asked. "You? Miller? Gus Olsen?"

Wojensky managed to repress a smile and answer simply, "First Sergeant Ben Cohen."

Malone moaned and lay back on his bunk. If there had been any chance that this duty might turn into a fling, that killed it. Cohen stood for no nonsense and tended to get a little hot if anyone tried to kick up a little. Duty was duty with Cohen, although once upon a time Malone and the big sergeant had gotten drunk in town, sharing three fifths of whiskey. That had been a hell of a night. Cohen had whipped Malone's ass, but he had done it in a friendly fashion, and when it was done they got back to their drinking. But that was off duty, and there was a hell of a difference in Ben Cohen's mind, although to Malone that line was razor-thin.

"It's all clear to me," Wojensky said. "Wherever Ben Cohen goes, you go. He wants to keep an eye on you, Malone. Just what in hell did you do, anyway?"

"I don't know." Malone sagged back again, recalling the night he had been drunk. Saturday night? What in hell had he done to make Cohen angry? He sighed and rolled over, deciding that despite its obvious blessings, alcohol may be the curse others accused it of being.

"Corson?"

Corson opened an eye to see Pettigrew hunched over him. "No. Go away."

"I have to get out tonight. I have to see her, to tell her," Pettigrew insisted.

"No. We damn near got caught last time. Not again."

Pettigrew's friendship wasn't worth a dressing down or a month on the punishment roster.

"Please!" Pettigrew pleaded, but Corson pretended to be asleep and there was nothing Pettigrew could do except creep back to his own bunk and stare at the ceiling in worry, or sleep, dreaming of soft lips, full breasts, and ten elusive horses galloping across the endless plains.

five _____

The molten sun poured down on his back from out of the clear sky. Andy Pettigrew, waist-deep in the new latrine pit, glanced up, seeing not the low, wispy clouds far to the west, but the figure of a reclining woman, soft and inviting. He stood there watching as the wind slowly rearranged his imagination's object.

"Are you nuts?" Malone sagged back against the wall of the pit. "A hundred and fifty-five degrees, and you're standing there smiling. Pettigrew!"

"What is it, Malone?" Pettigrew asked dreamily.

Malone's answer was a grumbling mutter. He gazed at Pettigrew in wonder. Here he was, within two months of discharge, and now his mind was going on him. It was ironic.

"Did you ever do any mustanging?" Pettigrew asked.

Malone stopped his digging again, and faced Pettigrew across the waist-deep pit.

"Wild horses?"

"Yes."

"No, never did any of that. If you remember Shy Whitaker, he was up from Colorado, and he'd done some of it."

"But you worked as a cowboy."

"Once long ago and never again," Malone said wryly.

"But you can use a rope."

"Pettigrew, are you asking me something, or is this a guessing game? Maybe you're after my life story."

"I'm asking about wild horses, Malone."

"Around here?" The sweat trickled into Malone's eyes, stinging them, and he wiped it away.

"Yes." Hesitantly, Pettigrew began telling Malone his problem. Once into the story he rushed along, his face distorted with emotion. "I've got to have those horses, you see, or lose her to Black Hatchet. That was him you saw yesterday, watching me."

"That buck? Wondered what made him so interested in a latrine pit."

"So you see why I've been asking you about wild horses."

Malone shook his head. "You came to the wrong man, Andy. Far as I know, nobody in this outfit has done any of that kind of work."

"But you *could* do it."

"Could?" Malone laughed. "No. When would I do that? How? What do you have in mind, riding out onto the plains and rounding up wild ponies? Think the Cheyenne and Sioux would let you get away with that? Those horses, brands or no, belong to the Indians—that's the way they figure it, anyway. They'd take it mighty hard, Pettigrew."

"But if a couple of men—"

"Wait." Malone held up his hand. "If a man—one

man—was to somehow rope and gentle ten mustangs under the noses of the hostiles, just what in hell would he do with them? Keep them under his bed in the barracks? Can't be done, Pettigrew. I know you're looking for some way out of your predicament, but that just ain't it. It would take a half-dozen experienced mustangers with a place to hold the ponies, with something to feed them. It would take men who weren't otherwise occupied digging latrine pits and saluting blue uniforms." Malone had started to lift his pick when Pettigrew spoke again.

"I thought," Andy said, "well, we're going to be out with Lord Whitechapel. Maybe there won't be a lot for us to do. I heard there's still mustangs over near the Medicine Bows. I thought—"

"Andy," Malone said roughly, "quit thinking."

The day grew no cooler as the sun floated toward its zenith. It glared down mockingly. Malone and Pettigrew chipped away at the hard earth. Malone's temper was getting short by the time a long shadow fell across the floor of the pit and he looked up to see a man in a dark suit and bowler hat standing over them.

"I say, what is this?"

The accent was British, the face long and sallow, with a hooked nose. Malone was in no mood for hands across the sea.

"It's a wishing well," he grumbled.

"Really? How unique. Indian custom, is it?"

Malone took off his hat and stood panting, sweat drenching his body. He stared up at the Englishman, wondering if the man could possibly be serious.

He decided he was. Malone had never seen a man he could read at first glance like this one. Absolutely without a sense of humor, self-important, stiff and unbending.

"I'll have to speak to His Lordship," the Englishman

48

said. "Perhaps it would amuse him to have a Cheyenne wishing well dug for him."

"Maybe he could just come over and visit this one when he feels the urge," Malone grunted.

"Perhaps. I'm looking for Malone and Pettigrew," the man said, giving each name a sort of fruity interpretation as he rolled them off his tongue.

"You are? You've found them, but who the hell are you."

"I am Reginald Dolittle. You shall have to call me Mr. Dolittle. I am the household manager."

"Fine." Malone started back to work.

"I wanted to notify you that you will be in the scullery." Dolittle said, still standing erect in the hot sun, his face expressionless.

"We will what?" Malone asked.

"Scullery?" Pettigrew finally joined the conversation, leaving his imaginary horses for a moment.

"Yes, it's an area where we are particularly short, just at the moment. Mr. Baggott and Miss Coombs ran out on us in Laramie, with some idea of getting married and living in America, I think." Dolittle made a face which demonstrated strong disapproval. "The scullery, as a result, is shorthanded. This will be your area of responsibility."

"Now just a fuckin' minute!" Malone exploded. He might have climbed out of the pit, but Pettigrew put a hand on his arm and shook his head.

"You mean," Pettigrew asked, "that Private Malone and I will be scrubbing pots for His Lordship?"

"Precisely that. Succinctly put."

Malone looked as if he would like to place his fist succinctly in Dolittle's face. Pettigrew felt him ease up a little, however. "Shit, KP again," was all he said.

Dolittle made a little bow and was gone, Malone glaring after him. Pettigrew looked miserable.

"No mustangs in the scullery, huh?" Malone said.

"No." And no mustangs meant no Dawn Fox. Pettigrew's last feeble hope was fading away like morning mist.

"Cohen," Malone was mumbling. "Cohen's got me on his list. Why? What in hell did I do Saturday night?" He was determined to find out.

All Malone could recall was walking over to Pop's store to have a few beers with McBride, Rafferty, Stretch Dobbs, and Holzer. A few beers. He had been sitting listening to the jawing—Rafferty was telling some tale no one believed about a rich uncle in Kansas—just listening, watching the fuzz develop around the lanterns as the alcohol worked on his brain.

There had been two civilians, buffalo hunters, sitting in the corner, playing a game of checkers. Pop Evans was there, of course, looking harried and greedy. Holzer was rambling on in German. Some poem, it seemed to be. He recalled Lieutenant Fitzgerald, who had been OD, poking his head in, saying good evening, and leaving.

But that was all. After that, everything seemed to be hidden in a fuzzy alcoholic haze.

Malone sighed, peered at the sun from out of his "wishing well," and got to work.

"All packed?"

Ben Cohen looked around from his duffle which rested on the somewhat worn sofa in his quarters. He turned and met the laughing blue eyes of his Irish lady, Maggie Cohen.

"Just about. It's been so long since I was in the field for any length of time, I've forgotten what a man needs."

50

"What you seem to need most, you won't find in the field, Ben Cohen," Maggie said.

"Saucy today, aren't we?"

"A little. The truth is, Ben Cohen, I hate to see you going. But I suppose you need it. You've been just a bear to live with lately."

"Woman! What do you mean? I've been just as sweet and lovable as ever! If you think, goddammit, that I've been . . ." Cohen stopped and smiled sheepishly. He spread his arms and welcomed Maggie into them. "Well, maybe a little restless."

"A *little*?"

"Maybe I shouldn't go. How's Gus Olsen going to handle this outfit? What's he know about being first sergeant? The men will run rings around him, be up to their old tricks in no time."

"Ben, Gus Olsen is a fine and competent soldier. He'll be no Ben Cohen, but he'll hold down the job well enough, and you know it."

"Yes, I know it." He kissed her forehead and hugged her more tightly with his bearlike arms.

Maggie kissed him on the lips, stretching on tiptoes to do it. She studied his broad, strong face, the face that kept the enlisted men quaking in their boots. But just now she saw only a strong, gruff man whose heart was made of gold.

"You don't mind if I go?" he asked.

"Of course I mind, man. You big ox, I'll miss you, but it's orders now, isn't it?"

"It's orders." He had begun slowly unbuttoning her dress and she stood smiling, shrugging her shoulders free to help him. Ben Cohen picked her up in his massive arms and carried to the bed. It was time to begin saying goodbye in a proper way.

51

• • •

Friday morning dawned clear and cold, the eastern skies a quick flush of rose-violet. The plains were stained purple. The grass was silver with dew. Lieutenant Matt Kincaid rode at the head of the small patrol, approaching the head of the column, where Lord Whitechapel, in a fur-collared coat, sat his sleek black horse, waiting.

His party was packed and ready. The tents had been collapsed and folded, the camp stoves packed, the oxen and horses harnessed, the silver and china carefully put away.

"Morning, Kincaid. Nice to see you." Whitechapel nodded but proffered no hand.

"Good morning, sir. This is Sergeant Ben Cohen."

Whitechapel nodded curtly again. Democracy was all well and good, but one couldn't carry enfranchisement into the enlisted ranks.

Cohen's face held its professional inexpressiveness. Matt Kincaid shifted in his McClellan saddle to see the black, enclosed wagon drawing up. On the driver's seat was the red-liveried, mustached man Kincaid had noticed before, and beside him sat Lady Virginia Whitechapel, wearing a sealskin jacket, a divided green skirt, soft brown boots, and a broad-brimmed white hat.

"Good morning, gentlemen," she said.

"Good morning, Lady Whitechapel."

"I thought," the earl said, leaping in, "that we should follow the stream until it joins the Powder River, then move southward toward the Medicine Bows."

"We might be better off striking out across country," Kincaid said. "There are a lot of coulees to the south along the creek."

"My man says there's not enough water," Lord White-chapel said. His tone seemed to end the discussion, so Kincaid fell silent. "Here! Stonebrook!"

52

Kincaid's eyes shifted to a suede-clad man with a straw hat, who was now drifting toward their party. "My gamekeeper," Lord Whitechapel said, by way of introduction.

"How d'you do?" the gamekeeper said, flashing a gap-toothed smile. "William Stonebrook's the name. Lieutenant Kincaid?"

"Yes, I am." He took Stonebrook's hand.

"The lieutenant wants to strike out across country, Stonebrook," Whitechapel said. The earl went into a long verbal detour. "Stonebrook's been with me in India and South Africa. He's my gamekeeper. I suppose you'd call him a scout. Damn good one, too. Dead shot. Eyes of a red Indian. Trust him implicitly."

"What's the reason for striking out across country, Lieutenant?" Stonebrook asked with sincere interest.

"The land's pretty well broken up with coulees along the creek southward," Matt told him. "Getting the wagons across will present some problems."

"Water," Lord Whitechapel put in. The man looked slightly irritated. Kincaid glanced back at the outpost. They weren't even out of sight of it yet, and already there were problems, although Stonebrook seemed candid and amenable to suggestions.

"His Lordship means that there doesn't seem to be enough water to the east to support his considerable aggregation of livestock," Stonebrook said. He removed his straw hat and wiped back his thinning crop of reddish hair.

"You've been east?"

Stonebrook nodded. "I had a look round. Seemed to me water might be a problem."

"I can assure you there is enough in isolated pools to water the stock," Kincaid said. "It might take a little wandering around, but we'll still be making better time

53

that way than trying to follow the creek."

"Buffalo," Lord Whitechapel barked, leaving it to Stonebrook to explain again.

"His Lordship means that I came across a large herd of bison twenty miles south along the creek, Lieutenant Kincaid. Quite a number of them, perhaps five hundred. Lord Whitechapel is eager to be at them."

"I see."

"And that obviously settles matters, doesn't it?" Lord Whitechapel boomed.

"Sir?"

"I am here to hunt, sir, not to detour around obstacles which stand between myself and my game. South it is, gentlemen. Along the creek."

With that, Lord Whitechapel raked the flanks of his black with a pair of rowelless silver spurs and moved off, holding himself erect in the saddle, using both hands on the reins.

Stonebrook gave Kincaid a glance that might have been sympathetic and set out to catch up with the earl.

"How in blazes he plans on making those coulees with these wagons, I don't know," Cohen said.

"We'll have to find out, Ben. It doesn't matter what our doubts are, does it? It's southward, along the creek. As Lord Whitechapel says, it's settled. And in the same manner I expect everything else to be settled on this hunt," he added.

Before ordering his detail forward, Kincaid looked back once again toward Outpost Number Nine, wistfully watching the flag flutter in the morning breeze.

six ———————————————

    The expedition didn't make it far that first day. As Kincaid had explained, the land along the creek to the south was broken with coulees. Winter rains rushing toward the creek cut deep gouges in the land. Slope-sided, sandy-bottomed gorges ran to the creek, which flowed between high bluffs.

It was impossible to take the wagons along the narrow beaches fronting the creek, and impossible as well to take the wagons through the coulees, which formed a network of interlocking trenches.

Or so Kincaid believed. Lord Whitechapel wasn't so easily dissuaded. He had said southward, and southward it would be.

Kincaid was close behind Lady Whitechapel's wagon as the driver drew up before a thirty-foot-deep gouge in the floor of the plains.

Behind Kincaid the ox-drawn wagons and the pony

carts drew up in orderly file. Matt rode to the edge of the coulee, where Stonebrook stood holding the reins of his horse. He shook his head doubtfully.

"What's holding us up, man?" Whitechapel boomed.

"The canyon, sir," Stonebrook answered.

"It's not the Khyber Pass, for God's sake. Beat down a ramp, Stonebrook. Beat down a ramp."

"Yes, Your Lordship," Stonebrook answered. He glanced at Kincaid and mounted his horse, gathering Lord Whitechapel's men.

"What about us, sir?" Ben Cohen asked.

"I suppose we'd better lend a hand," Kincaid said without enthusiasm. "Start crumbling the bank, spread it, and try to build some sort of a ramp. God knows, we'll be lucky if we don't spill a couple of wagons and end this expedition right here."

"That would be a pity," Cohen replied, straightfaced. He turned to the patrol. "Camp shovels! You heard the Lieutenant. We're going to build a little ramp down into the coulee for the wagons. When we're done with that, we'll build another little ramp up the far side. Get a move on. Malone, hop to it! Quit moping."

Malone was grumbling something to the effect that the army should have just issued him a shovel and forgotten his rifle. Holzer was already at the edge of the coulee, tentatively trying to cave in the banks with a boot. By the time Fremont, Rafferty, and Corson joined him, Stonebrook had arrived with two dozen of Whitechapel's men.

It didn't take long to beat down a ramp and pack the earth with the horses hooves, but their best job left a steep declivity, and that sandy earth just didn't pack well.

"We'll need lines, Sergeant," Kincaid said, and Ben set out to find some. Naturally, Whitechapel was nowhere in sight. Likely he was off seeing if the champagne was chilled yet.

His lady *was* there.

"Hot work for the men," she said, and Matt turned to find her standing behind him, a smile on her pink lips, her green eyes dancing, her honey-blonde hair drifting in the breeze.

"Yes, Lady Whitechapel. There's not a breath of wind in the coulee."

"This doesn't appear to have been the wisest course," she said, bending forward at the waist to peer into the coulee. "Is it safe?"

"I wouldn't recommend riding in the wagon, Lady Whitechapel. If the wheels hit a soft spot, the wagon will heel over and possibly roll."

"You don't have to say that, Lieutenant."

"Pardon me?"

"'Lady Whitechapel' is awfully formal. We'll be together most of the summer. Call me Virginia."

As she said that, she stepped closer to him and placed her hand on Kincaid's arm. Those eyes were doing more than dancing just then. Kincaid saw and recognized an invitation. He also saw, across her shoulder, Lord White-chapel returning astride his black charger.

"Got to see to my men," Kincaid mumbled, turning quickly away. "How's it going, Sergeant Cohen?" he shouted needlessly. Ben, wiping his brow, looked up with some puzzlement and then simply spread his arms. Kincaid waved a hand negligently.

Turning back, he found that Lady Whitechapel—Virginia—had sauntered off and the earl sat his horse, staring down into the coulee.

"Not over yet?" he asked. "Costly delay, Kincaid."

"Yes, sir."

"Not fair to blame your men, I suppose. You're only a handful. But the British Corps of Engineers, I assure you, would have had us across by now."

Kincaid muttered that he supposed they would have, excused himself, and went to where Stonebrook, Malone, and Rafferty were tying lines onto the enclosed wagon.

"What do you think, sir?" Stonebrook asked.

"I think we had better take it damned easy. Can the regular driver handle this?"

"Winston? Yes, sir." Stonebrook's eyes crinkled into a smile. "You'd be surprised at some of the situations he's been in, sir."

Rafferty and Malone mounted and looped a dally around each of their saddles. On the off-side, two of Lord Whitechapel's men, both obviously Americans, did the same. Stonebrook spoke to Winston, who still sat looking splendid in his red livery, as if he were off for a drive through Kensington Park, and the wagon lurched forward.

Winston let the front wheels roll over the embankment before he locked the brake on hard. The wagon immediately began to slide sideways, but the British driver had no choice. That wagon was as heavy as a freight rig, and there was no way the four additional horses were going to keep it from careening out of control down the cut.

Malone had his horse practically on its haunches. The line to the rear axle of the wagon was taut and straining. He saw the wagon teeter on the edge of the embankment and plunge over. With amazement he saw that the wagon was still upright. As it rolled on in spumes of dust, heeling to the left and then the right, the horses wild-eyed, the driver expressionless, Malone realized that the damned thing was actually going to make it down in one piece.

Malone sat his shuddering horse, watching as the lines below were untied and the enclosed wagon pulled free of the foot of the ramp.

"What do you think?"

Malone turned to find Ben Cohen beside him, sleeves rolled up over massive forearms.

"What I think is that if those freight wagons are any heavier, we'll never make it this way. There's no decent way to dally a rope on a McClellan saddle."

"Uh-huh," was all Cohen said. He was looking at the converted Conestogas that carried Lord Whitechapel's "necessities." Then he ambled to where Kincaid stood watching.

"Sir, we can't do it this way. Maybe if we unhitched the second ox team and used them to draw in the other direction as the wagon descends?"

"Use your judgment, Ben."

"Wait a minute, Kincaid," Whitechapel said. "That's going to waste a hell of a lot of time."

"We're liable to lose a man this way, sir."

"Well . . ." Whitechapel mumbled into his mustache. He looked at Ben Cohen as if deciding whether losing a man or two really mattered, then grumped, "Talk to Stonebrook. Do it in the manner most suitable."

With that the earl was gone, and Kincaid remarked, "Wonder how the British Engineer Corps would do this?"

"Sir?"

"Nothing, Ben. Find Stonebrook and tell him what you want to do."

Stonebrook was agreeable, happy to have the suggestion, it seemed. It worked fairly well. With a team of oxen pulling in the opposite direction to act as an efficient if temperamental brake, they managed to get the heavy wagon down in one piece.

Slowly the entire caravan was let down into the coulee

and, with much struggling and a lot of towing, drawn up the far side. The horse herd was brought through last, to the accompaniment of barking dogs and yelling wranglers, amid mountainous clouds of dust.

The crossing had taken a little less than two hours.

They managed to make three more miles before they reached the next coulee.

It was there that a dour Lord Whitechapel caught up with Kincaid.

"Lieutenant, I've been an ass. How many more of these damnable things—coulees—are there?"

"At least a dozen, sir."

"At this rate we'll be lucky to make ten miles in the next two days." Whitechapel shook his head and Kincaid thought the corner of his silver mustache lifted in a faint smile. "Been an ass, as I say. I ought to know enough to listen to the locals. Always been a bit stubborn. Apologize. Talk to Stonebrook, will you, Kincaid? Set our course as you see fit."

"Figure it out, did he?" Ben Cohen asked after Whitechapel had ridden away.

"Yes. And he apologized. It's not easy for a man like Whitechapel to admit he's wrong, Ben. I admire him for it."

"I'd have admired him more if he'd admitted it a little sooner," Cohen said.

Matt found Stonebrook and told him, "We're going to turn east and get out of the coulees before we veer off toward the Medicine Bows."

"Good. We wouldn't have made it far without losing a wagon and maybe some men." Stonebrook turned to a lean man in Western clothes. "You heard that, Ernie. Get 'em moving east."

There was still an hour of daylight left when they made camp. A tiny ribbon of a stream flowed through the stubbled hillocks to the east. Lord Whitechapel's people had the wooden-sided tents up within thirty minutes, and in forty-five minutes there was smoke rising from the portable stove in the cook's tent.

"Lamb," Malone said. "Lamb and baked apples. Lamb, baked apples, and biscuits." He sat on the ground with his back against his saddle, sniffing the air, trying to identify each aroma drifting from the cook's tent. Although half of it was imagination, it was enough to stir up the juices. Fremont had been chosen as camp cook for the soldiers, and he stirred the beans again, then rose to cross to his pack and fetch the cheesecloth-wrapped side of bacon, which he began shaving into a frying pan.

"Lamb and baked apples, biscuits and honey . . ."

"You can't smell honey from here," Rafferty said.

"I can't see the man having biscuits without honey," Malone said logically. "Or marmalade, maybe. Lamb, baked apples, hot biscuits with marmalade . . ."

"Shut up, Malone," Fremont growled.

Malone's eyes lifted to the big man, who was wiping his bacon knife off on his trousers.

"Lamb and baked apples, biscuits and *marmalade*, pheasant and truffles."

"What the hell's truffles?" Corson asked.

"I don't know. All those Englishman eat them. Lamb and baked apples . . ."

"Goddammit, Malone!" Fremont came out of his crouch, the knife still in his hands. "Don't you ever stop that jabbering?"

"Lamb!" Malone counted on his fingers. He never got to baked apples. Fremont charged across the camp, his knife going up, and Malone rolled away, coming to his feet.

Pettigrew, too, was in motion. He lunged, diving for Fremont's ankles, and the big man went down before he

61

could reach Malone. Rafferty and Holzer were on Fremont's back now, Rafferty bending back Fremont's hand to force the knife free.

"What in hell is going on here!" the all-too-familiar voice boomed.

Malone turned his head to find Sergeant Cohen standing, hands on hips, glowering at them. "Nothing," he muttered automatically.

"Nothing!" Cohen walked to where Rafferty stood, knife in hand. "These things kill, boys." He took the knife. "I won't stand for this shit. Whatever the problem is, bury it! That's an order. Malone, Pettigrew, get your butts down to the cook's tent. Find a Mr. Dolittle and report to him."

"Yes, Sarge." Malone picked up his hat and dusted his shirt front off.

"Damn you, Malone," Fremont panted. "You and that Indian-loving son of a bitch with you."

"Shut up," Ben Cohen said, and Fremont shut his mouth, sitting, hands hanging against the earth.

"I hope they feed us down there," Malone said as he and Pettigrew walked toward Lord Whitechapel's camp. "Hope they feed us real well. Hope they give us lamb and baked apples..."

"Stay away from that man, Fremont," Ben Cohen told the soldier after Malone had disappeared. "He's a pain in the ass, but he's tough enough to make two of you."

"He hasn't shown me that yet," Fremont puffed, coming to his feet.

"No, and I don't *want* him showing you. You've been trouble since you transferred, Fremont. I don't think there's anyone you can get along with. What's with you and Pettigrew, anyway?"

"Son of a bitch is an Indian-lover."

"That's all? Rafferty!" Cohen roared.

"Me?"

"We have two Raffertys here? What's the story?"

"I don't know." Rafferty shrugged. "Pettigrew likes an Indian, Fremont don't like people who like Indians. They've scuffled."

"No more. There won't be any more 'scuffling.' I mean it. You'll have me to buck next time, Fremont, and I don't think you'd like the result of that."

Fremont didn't think so, either. Cohen's arms were the size of an average man's legs. His barrel chest would put a grizzly to shame.

"All right, Sergeant," he said quietly.

Cohen held out the bacon knife. "You know what this utensil is for?"

"Yes, Sergeant."

Cohen slapped it against Fremont's palm and walked off into the gathering twilight. He wanted nothing more right now than to rinse off in the stream and to fill his belly with those beans, which everyone else seemed to hold in contempt.

He wouldn't have admitted it, but Cohen was weary and sore. It was a long time since he had sat a saddle all day. Now he wanted only a quick rinse-off, a meal, and a night's sleep.

That was all Kincaid wanted as well, but he had an officer's obligations. He was to dine with His Lordship and party. That included Lady Virginia. Trouble she was, if Kincaid was reading her right. Beautiful and all too tempting. That was all he needed. Any trouble with Lady Virginia would lead to diplomatic hell. Via State Department, via War . . .

Still, she was a hell of a fine-looking woman. . . . Kincaid shook the thought off and, with a sigh, straightened his tunic and strode toward the huge tent where Lord Alvin Whitechapel was preparing to dine.

There were two people there whom Kincaid had not met. Where they had been keeping themselves was a mystery. The young woman with the overly ambitious nose and receding chin was introduced as Suzanne Ridgeley.

"My charming niece," Lord Whitechapel said, beaming. Kincaid bowed and kissed the extended hand of Suzanne Ridgeley, producing a simpering coo from the woman's lips. She blinked at Kincaid in a way that made him think she was myopic.

"And her fiancé, Benjamin Doyle."

Kincaid shook the dry hand of the young man. Doyle was tall, with rounded shoulders, and fair-haired—a bit of pink scalp was already showing through the curls— blue-eyed and apparently nervous. The corner of his eye jerked in response to a hectic tic.

"Shall we dine?" Virginia Whitechapel asked. "Won't you sit by me, Lieutenant Kincaid?"

"Happily," Kincaid said, less than happily. He was seated next to her, and although Whitechapel seemed indifferent, Kincaid didn't like it much. He was near enough to distinguish her soft scent above the smell of the food, which the serving maids were now bringing in to place on the candlelit table.

When she moved, her ruffled dress brushed against Kincaid's leg, and when Her Ladyship bent to pick up a napkin that had somehow fallen to the floor, Kincaid was given an awesome view of perfect white cleavage rising into tantalizing white breasts.

"I can be clumsy," Virginia Whitechapel said, her eyes twinkling as she looked at Matt Kincaid, who was trying to imitate a wooden Indian.

Kincaid decided it would be a good idea to take another tack. He asked Suzanne Ridgeley, "How is it we haven't met before, Miss Ridgeley?"

She looked up slowly, blinking her nearsighted eyes. Her face was blank for a moment. "I haven't been well, Lieutenant. Change in climate, you know. Benjamin has been taking care of me. I've been abed in the wagon."

"I trust you are feeling better now." Kincaid could feel Lady Whitechapel's eyes on him, *feel* her smile.

"Oh, rather. Benjamin is quite a healer." Then she blushed furiously and buried her face in a napkin.

Kincaid glanced at Whitechapel, but his lordship was still silent, distracted by his meal, which he seemed to be enjoying immoderately. It was very good, in fact, as Kincaid discovered when he himself was served—simple but tasty. Lamb and baked apples, hot biscuits with honey and marmalade.

seven _____

Malone was elbow-deep in soapy water, a cigar clenched between his teeth, a string of muttered curses spilling out from between his compressed lips.

"Everything all right, Mr. Malone?"

Malone looked around to see Dolittle, neat as a pin in a white jacket and white tie.

"Fine. It looks to me like you've got enough people here to take care of these pots without dragging us in, Dolittle. Why us?"

"Enough help?" Dolittle shook his head at Malone's ignorance. "His Lordship is down to ten serving people. As you may or may not know, two servants abandoned us at Laramie."

"Two smart ones," Malone said around his cigar stub.

"I thought soldiers never complained of their duties," Dolittle said in that fruity tone of his.

"You ain't known many soldiers, then. What about

her?" Malone lifted his chin toward an overweight, red-faced woman who was sitting in a wooden chair across the twenty-by-twenty room.

"Hilda's a chambermaid."

"And her?" he asked, indicating a prim, plain young woman who was carrying a tray.

"Betsy? She's a serving maid. Couldn't possibly ask her to double in scullery!"

"No." Malone examined the black iron pot he was washing, grumbled, and immersed it in the soapy water. "Say, Dolittle, we haven't gotten a bite to eat yet."

"You will be fed," Dolittle said reassuringly, "as soon as the master is finished."

"Yeah? What?"

"Excuse me, Mr. Malone?"

"*Private* Malone. Last time someone called me 'mister,' I was still a happy man. What I mean is, what do we eat?"

"It is usual to have whatever His Lordship has eaten," Dolittle said. "There's little sense in preparing two meals, after all."

"Oh, yeah?" Malone was suddenly interested. "Wouldn't include lamb, would it?"

Dolittle told him exactly what it included, down to the wine. "Not too much, just a drop, of course. Can't have the help stumbling about."

"Dolittle, you're not such a pain in the ass. Come on, Pettigrew, get with it. Supper's waiting."

Pettigrew didn't hurry up; in fact, he hadn't heard Malone. He heard nothing but the soft whispering of a woman who was not there, who lay far away on this night, perhaps stalked by Black Hatchet, and Pettigrew simply worked on methodically, his worried thoughts far distant.

"Malone, is it?"

67

Malone looked up from his meal—or what had been a meal. It was now only an empty plate ringed by a few sprigs of parsley. When he looked up, his gaze was met by a pair of deep blue, merry eyes, by a freckled face peering out from beneath a bonnet of red hair.

"I'm Malone."

"I could see the map of Kilkenny all over your ugly face," the girl said. "Me, I'm Mary McGuire. Late of County Cork, now in service to this British profligate, to my own shame."

Malone hadn't suffered such a flamboyant greeting in a while. His mind had still been on the lamb when Mary McGuire, all four-foot-eleven of her, had appeared out of the blue, with her mop of red Irish hair and her freckled nose, her serving uniform that couldn't hide the exuberance of her fully bloomed figure and her ready smile.

"You know my name," he said finally.

"A proud soldier like you in the scullery." She sat beside him on the bench at the servant's table, bumping him aside with her hip. "It's a shame and a downright pity, it is. An Irish lad and a fighting man, scourge of the heathen Indians, washing dishes for an Englishman!" she spat dryly.

"It's the life," Malone shrugged.

"Sure and it is. That's the sad truth." Malone leaned back against the wall, remembering too late that it was only canvas, and only Mary McGuire's hand placed quickly on his knee kept him from toppling over backward.

After he had recovered his balance, the hand remained on his knee and Malone smiled, suddenly liking this job.

"All right! All right!" Dolittle appeared, clapping his hands. "It's time to finish the washing now. Watch your work. It's been a little haphazard."

Sighing, Malone rose. He pondered telling Dolittle in

clinical detail what he could do with the dishes, but decided against it. Orders.

However far afield this job was from his regular duties, he was still under orders, although he would dearly have liked to remind Dolittle that he wasn't one of His Lordship's goddamn servants.

"They're all the same, these Englishmen," Mary McGuire whispered. "Not you. Not you, Malone."

Her breath was close and pleasant against Malone's ear. He felt a slow stirring begin in his loins, and he looked at the redheaded Irish girl intently, trying to decide whether it was imagination.

It wasn't.

She stood hipshot, a hand at her waist, tapping a toe. Her blue eyes positively flashed, and her freckled face split into a wide grin. She turned then and jounced away, hips swinging, smiling back across her shoulder, a freckled sprite.

"The pots, Malone."

"All right," he said, scowling his best scowl at Dolittle. It bounced off him, and Malone wished that Dolittle were neck-deep in that "wishing well," which ought to be good and ripe by now.

Kincaid was bidding his host good evening. Lord Whitechapel seemed a little the worse for the wear. It could have been the brandy that polished off the meal, following the claret and sauterne that had accompanied the earlier courses.

The rest of the party escorted Matt out into the evening, which was warm yet, roofed over by a flawless, star-filled sky.

Lady Whitechapel walked far too close to Kincaid, followed by the engaged couple, Suzanne and Benjamin Doyle. Looking at Suzanne, Kincaid wondered what would possess a man to court her. Possibly her connection with a titled gentleman and the monetary benefits that would accrue to her as a result.

It surely wasn't animal magnetism. The nearsighted Suzanne was a nice enough woman, if a bit dull-witted, but she wasn't the type to drive men mad.

Which was not the case with Lady Virginia Whitechapel. She had grace and beauty, and simply exuded sexuality. Enough so that if Kincaid wasn't being driven mad, he was at least being made definitely uncomfortable.

Again he turned his attention to Suzanne Ridgeley, not wanting any hints of romance filtering back to Lord Whitechapel. Via Whitechapel via State via War via Conway.

"A lovely evening," he said to Suzanne, who blinked twice, as if looking around to determine who had been speaking to her.

"Yes. I love the evenings out here," her nasal voice responded. "The big American sky."

Matt nodded. He hadn't thought of it in those terms, but he supposed he liked the big American sky as well. "It's a grand evening for a walk," Virginia said, taking Kincaid's arm suddenly.

"Might be a bit dangerous, eh, Kincaid?" Benjamin Doyle put in.

"Dangerous?" Kincaid grasped at that as Lady Whitechapel grasped at him. "Oh, yes. Savages. Wild animals. Rattlesnakes."

"At night, rattlesnakes?" Lady Whitechapel asked, amusement in her voice.

"Uh, occasionally," Kincaid answered. "I thought I heard a prowling cougar earlier."

"I thought they were only to be found nearer the mountains," Virginia said, gripping his arm still more tightly.

"I should love to take a stroll," Suzanne said wistfully.

"Good," Kincaid said hastily. "Shall we?"

He took her arm and guided her blindly into the darkness, walking quickly away from what he was sure was a mocking smile on the ripe and intriguing lips of Virginia Whitechapel.

With Benjamin Doyle close on their heels, Kincaid led the stumbling Suzanne along the narrow creek, wishing all the while that he dared view the wonders of the "big American sky" with the lady with the laughing eyes.

Malone, meanwhile, had stumbled on another sort of wonder.

"Where are you taking all that water?" he asked Mary McGuire.

"To Mr. Farnsworth, of course," she said, lifting the iron kettle from the fire.

"Who's he?"

"Mr. Farnsworth? He's the camp manager, of course. And Lord Whitechapel's personal valet."

"Guess I haven't seen him." Malone took a dishcloth and wrapped it around the handle of the boiling pot. "Give me that, Shorty, you'll scald yourself."

Mary started to flare up, but saw the grin on Malone's face and smiled.

"What's Farnsworth want with all this hot water anyway?" Malone asked.

"It's not for Mr. Farnsworth, it's for the earl," Mary McGuire answered. "Would you like to see?"

"See what?"

"Come along." Mary was smiling devilishly. "We look all the time, me and the girls."

"Look at what?"

"Come along. If you will carry the pot. Come along now, my lad."

She crooked her finger and Malone followed her

71

through the canvas flap that led to the outside of the cook's tent, then along the side of the wooden-walled main tent to a secondary door.

"You'll have to give me the pot now," Mary said. "Mr. Farnsworth won't like it awfully much if he sees you doing for me."

Malone handed over the heavy pot filled with boiling water, which Mary handled with surprising ease. There was a lot of strength packed into that diminutive frame, he decided.

Mary put a finger to her lips and Malone backed away into the shadows as she rapped on the tent frame and the door opened to reveal a stout, redfaced man who took the kettle without saying a word and closed the door again.

Mary rushed to where Malone stood waiting, baffled. "That's it?"

"No. Hush, we have to wait a few minutes. Come over here." She led the way around the corner of the tent, and Malone crept through the shadows after her.

"What?" he whispered.

Mary's answer was to turn and leap into his arms, her soft, cuddly body going against his, to plant a wet, warm kiss on his lips and draw back.

"You'll see."

Malone was already beyond caring. He stood beside her, letting his hand slip around her waist to cup her breast through the fabric of her uniform. Mary McGuire seemed to take no notice of it.

Malone had bent to kiss the nape of her neck beneath her pinned-up hair when she moved suddenly, rapping her skull against his nose.

"Now," she said.

"Now? Here?" Malone turned her, groping at her.

"Not that," she said, a laugh in her voice. "Here."

Malone crept forward and found a small split in the seam of the tent. Mary was holding a finger up for silence. She looked in and then gestured frantically for Malone to have a peek.

He did.

Inside the wooden-walled tent was a contraption made of impregnated canvas. Steam rose from it as Lord Whitechapel, walking toward the tub with great dignity, tested the water with his toe before allowing Farnsworth to remove his silk gown.

Then, white, naked, and thin, His Lordship stepped into the folding bathtub and lounged back, humming softly to himself as he washed his feet.

Mary had started giggling, and Malone had to pull her away quickly from the tent.

They ran twenty feet onto the dark grass and collapsed in a heap, Mary laughing and holding her stomach.

"That's what you do for laughs?" Malone asked in amazement.

"Yes. Don't you see, Malone, we see him all day prancing around in his fine clothes, his dignity intact. Then, when evening bath time comes, he stands there naked just like any other old man. It strips it all away—the awe of the man, I mean."

"I can think of jollier things to do," Malone said, bending low to kiss her throat. Mary was still shuddering with suppressed laughter. She could at least be serious about it, Malone thought.

"Every night," he said, sitting up himself, his head tilted back to look at the milky stars overhead. "I never heard of a man taking a bath every night. Out here! Living out of a tent!"

"Then you do see?"

"It's a wonder. I don't exactly see the humor in it," Malone said, "but it is something to wonder on."

"And this?"

Malone's head came around. Mary had unbuttoned the top of her dress, and her freckled breasts stood bare and full and proud beneath his gaze.

"Jesus," he muttered.

"Yes, Mr. Malone. Would you care to see the rest?"

It was all done by starlight, but Malone gave it a thorough looking-over while he undressed and Mary examined him. She was a well-rounded little thing, exuberant and practiced.

"Here, this way," she said, and she rolled away from Malone to go to her hands and knees. Malone crept up behind her, placing his hands on her smooth white buttocks as he drew her closer.

"Don't be shy, Mr. Malone," Mary said in a whispery, hurried voice. "Now. Please." Her hand wriggled frantically as she reached back and found Malone and settled him in her softness.

Malone sank into her to the hilt, his legs trembling. Mary had her head against the grass, her unpinned hair screening her face as her hips worked and her breathing became labored and shallow.

She deliberately slowed herself, and Malone heard her humming, definitely humming an old air as she swayed against him, becoming slowly more intent until Malone could stand it no longer, and he grabbed her thighs, pressing himself against her, feeling her last, almost frantic effort before he reached a hard, draining climax and fell forward against her back, clutching at her breasts, kissing her shoulder and back.

She lay beneath him, panting, the little Irish tune still rising from her throat as she quivered once more and lay still against the dewy grass.

Malone staggered back into camp an hour later, found his bedroll, and fell onto it. He lay back exhausted, pleased with himself and the world, staring at the stars floating overhead.

Ben Cohen saw him flop onto his bed, his boots still on, obviously worn out, and he wondered if maybe he wasn't laying it on Malone a bit thick. The man had ridden all day and washed dishes all night. Pettigrew had been back for a long while. Malone must have been stuck with the dirty work.

"Maybe," Cohen thought, "I'd better lighten up on him." With that noble thought still in his mind, Cohen too fell off to sleep, only once reaching over absently to search for Maggie before realizing she was far away on this evening.

Matt Kincaid wasn't sleeping. He doubted he would fall off to sleep this night. He had been trying, but closing his eyes only brought the face of Virginia Whitechapel nearer, made her lingering scent seem more vivid, the memory of her laughing eyes, her smooth white flesh return with intensity. And so he lay, eyes open, watching the stars, as did Andy Pettigrew, who was in as much, if not more, misery.

Andy watched the stars rise and shift, studying the constellations he knew. Andromeda, Orion, Pegasus . . . a winged horse as distant and unreachable as his own dream ponies.

He rolled over angrily and in frustration muttered once, "Dawn Fox."

eight ─────────

The hunting began in the morning. Shortly after ten they came upon the buffalo herd Stonebrook had spotted several days earlier. It was moving slowly southward, a dark brown mass against the green prairie.

"Hold up the train!" Lord Whitechapel said excitedly. "Rutledge, the weapons." His Lordship dismounted and stood, hands on hips, watching the creeping herd graze its way toward the distant mountains.

Matt Kincaid was at the earl's side, watching the tightly packed herd. A youth in a tight-fitting uniform had arrived with a small black case and he opened it for Whitechapel, who removed the brass-bound spyglass from it and slowly scanned the herd.

"There's a big old fellow—uh-oh, got his horn sheared off on the right side." Whitechapel shifted the glass, finally lighting on one he favored. "Big brute. Have a look, Kincaid. Far side, near the front. Next to the cow with the bad coat."

Kincaid dutifully took the glass and scanned the herd himself until he found the bull Whitechapel was interested in. "That's a lot of buffalo, that one," he said, handing the glass back.

"Wonder if it would match Lord Bertram's," Whitechapel mused out loud. "Can't tell from this distance, but look at that great shaggy head!"

Farnsworth had returned with the guns. Somehow Kincaid had expected a rifle case, perhaps two of them. What Farnsworth brought was positively amazing.

He had two helpers with him, and he and each of the helpers were carrying two specially made cases, six of them in all, and they placed them down next to His Lordship, who was still studying the herd.

The weapons in these cases were all heavy rifles, which made Kincaid assume there were still more weapons back in the tent. In one case rested two over-and-under heavy-bore rifles, one a Rigby with a gold-chased receiver, the engraving depicting Diana at the hunt. The stock was of bird's-eye maple, delicately carved, highly polished. The second rifle was of a make Kincaid didn't recognize, possibly a Westley Richards with silver scroll-work. Kincaid knew enough of guns to appreciate that that rifle cost about what he made in three years.

"What do you think, Kincaid? The .480, I think. Cartridges, Farnsworth."

Farnsworth stepped forward to give his lordship three heavy-caliber cartridges. The gun boy had uncased the Rigby and removed the sight hoods.

"From here?" Ben Cohen said skeptically. Kincaid shot him a glance. Kincaid's thoughts had held the same question. It was two hundred yards, slightly downslope, using iron tube sights. The bullet had enough punch to drop the buffalo from there, but not a man in a thousand could score a hit clean enough to kill at that range.

Lord Whitechapel, his pipe in his mouth, loaded the awesome weapon and shouldered it, tucking his right shoulder in close to his body.

He touched off, and the roar of the big-bore rifle rattled their eardrums. Smoke drifted across their field of vision. The buffalo herd milled a little, but did not run.

Sergeant Cohen, who had been watching this all with skepticism, arms folded, teeth clenched, now studied the herd, seeing no downed, thrashing animal.

"Missed the whole damned herd," Cohen muttered.

"Collect the head, Farnsworth. Have the skinners bring in the hide." His Lordship turned and handed the smoking weapon to his gun bearer.

Cohen still stood trying to hold back a smile. Suddenly he was no longer smiling. The milling herd had cleared away enough so that he could see the downed buffalo bull. It had been a clean, killing hit, taking the animal down instantly, and Cohen, eyes widening, turned to study the tall, mustached man who was calmly stoking up a pipe.

Doyle had appeared excitedly, waving his rifle around in the air. It was a Reilley .500 with enough foot-pounds of punch to stop an express train, and he was anxious to use it. The muzzle swung past Cohen, who leaped aside after a terrifying glance into that bore, which looked like the mouth of a cave.

"Look at them all!" Benjamin Doyle said excitedly. "Give me a dozen rounds, Jefferson."

"Best to wait until my skinners are out of there," Lord Whitechapel said.

"They'll scatter the herd!"

"Possibly. But if you stampede them, there's a chance

78

my head will be ruined. I won't have a trophy head ruined, Benjamin."

"No, sir," Doyle said. He lowered his rifle like a chastised, sulky child.

The herd had in fact begun to move away. Lord Whitechapel's skinners were moving up correctly, downwind, but the buffalo seemed to sense something. It wasn't enough to set them running, but they drifted southward.

"Horses, Farnsworth!" Lord Whitechapel called. "Alert the cart drivers."

"May I ask, sir," Kincaid said, "what it is we're doing?"

"Hunting, sir. Hunting." That was all Whitechapel would say. Kincaid sat his horse, watching. The herd had slowly drifted away from Lord Whitechapel's trophy bull, and now, as the horses were brought up, the earl mounted. Doyle was given a leg up onto a tall roan horse that appeared to be entirely too much animal for him. Kincaid fell in behind as the party moved to the southwest, keeping the buffalo herd on their flank, closing the range slightly.

Meanwhile, another party of riders had been sent across the creek to the west, and they were slowly moving in toward the opposite flank. A trio of carts had fallen in behind the herd, keeping a careful distance.

Farnsworth had fallen in beside Kincaid, carrying the rifle case. Cohen followed Kincaid, expressionless, silent.

"Here," Whitechapel said, and they halted near a low knoll that the herd must pass by. He dismounted, gave his horse's reins to a servant, called for his gun case, and loaded. Doyle, jittery with excitement, stood beside the earl.

"Kincaid?" His Lordship invited, nodding at the remaining guns.

"No, thank you, sir."

Whitechapel grunted something and took his shooting position. The riders on the far flank were gradually working the herd toward the knoll. Kincaid could see the skinners at work on the dead bull, see the carts a half-mile behind the slowly drifting herd.

"Near enough, Benjamin," Lord Whitechapel said. "Give them a sporting chance."

It wasn't much of a chance. Whitechapel opened up, scoring two kills with two shots. Doyle shot half the haunch off a bull, which dragged itself in a circle. Whitechapel reloaded and fired again, scoring one kill and one wounded, which set him to muttering in his mustache.

Doyle scored on his next shot, and again on his following round. Still the buffalo did not run. They had no idea what was happening.

Kincaid felt a light touch on his arm, and turned his head to find Lady Whitechapel standing beside him. She gripped his arm tightly, her eyes gleaming, and Kincaid did not try to take his arm away.

Whitechapel had switched weapons. The barrel of the Rigby was hot. He set to work efficiently with the new rifle, continuing to fire until the herd broke and ran, until the smoke rolled heavily across the plains and Kincaid's head throbbed with dull echoes.

A rough count by Kincaid tallied fifty buffalo dead on the plains as the skinners and carts moved in. Whitechapel handed his rifle to Fremont, who would clean and oil the rifles for His Lordship.

Whitechapel turned toward Kincaid, his eyes flickering only slightly as he noticed his wife's hands falling away from the lieutenant's arm.

"That's worked up an appetite," Whitechapel said. "Shall we return to the camp?"

"Yes," Kincaid said. "Whatever you say."

"The meat will be carted back to your outpost. That

will give your cook something to work with, eh?"

"It will indeed, sir," Kincaid said. He stepped into his stirrup and swung aboard his bay, wishing he was going back to Outpost Number Nine with the meat. They could just throw him onto one of the carts and haul him in.

"The man can shoot," Cohen said. "You've got to give him that."

Kincaid couldn't argue. He had never seen a better shot. The weapons, superior in every way, had something to do with it, but the man read distance and windage with a skill that indicated natural ability and long practice.

Kincaid asked the earl over luncheon if he didn't have one of those new telescopic sights.

"Have one—or had—threw the damned thing away! Unsportsmanlike, Kincaid. Rather be caught dead than admit that I took game with one of those toys."

After luncheon the earl decided to take a nap. Kincaid decided to remove himself from the tent. Virginia was making eyes at him again. Nice eyes. Deadly eyes. Would Lord Whitechapel settle himself in behind the sights and pick off a lover? Kincaid wondered. He decided that there was a very good possibility.

Ben Cohen watched Malone and Pettigrew straggle toward the cook's tent, and he called Malone over.

"Listen, Malone, I'm going to take you off this dishwashing detail. We'll rotate the duty among the men."

"Sarge," Malone said softly, "I know I done wrong. I want to make up for it. I don't want the other boys to have to take up my slack."

"Malone?" Cohen cocked his head. Was it that hot out here? "Is that you talking to me?"

"Yes, Sarge. I don't quite recall what it was I done

81

Saturday night, but I'm a big enough man to take my medicine. You just let me take my punishment. I'm offering no objections."

With that, Malone turned on his heel and was gone, leaving Ben Cohen to stand scratching his head. "Maybe the sun is getting to me," he muttered. Malone, taking the dirty duty without griping? Something was wrong somewhere. And what the hell was he talking about—Saturday night? What had that clown been up to? Cohen knew of nothing, but he decided that it would require some looking into, if it was enough to make Malone feel guilty.

Matt Kincaid nearly bumped into her. Coming around the corner of the tent, he had been looking at the ground, and he failed to notice the young lady until the last second.

"Miss Ridgeley."

"Yes?" She looked up and blinked. She was wearing a divided green skirt and a white blouse, her colorless hair pushed up into a ineffective arrangement.

"Sorry. I nearly bowled you over."

"Did you? I didn't notice. I was scanning the ground. Found this up on the knoll there, thought Uncle might be interested."

She handed Kincaid the small flint arrowhead, and he turned it over in his hand. "Very old, I think," Matt told her. "I've never seen Cheyenne or Sioux use anything like this. Possibly Arikara, though it's a bit far west for them."

"Arikara?"

"There used to be quite a number of them over east along the Upper Missouri, and there are still a few about. We've run into them from time to time."

"I've never heard of the tribe." They had begun walking slowly back toward the knoll where Suzanne Ridgeley had found the arrowhead.

"Their problem was they were a small nation. What happened to them is what usually happens to small nations. The big ones stepped on them. The whites pushed in from the east and the Sioux and Cheyenne overran them from the west. Ariks were never particularly liked by anyone. They have a peculiar and nasty habit."

"Oh?"

"Cannibalism," Kincaid told her. "It disgusted the Sioux. Every chance they got to attack an Arik camp, they generally took."

They stood on the knoll, the dry wind drifting past. Suzanne Ridgeley was bent nearly double, peering at the earth. "There must have been a camp here."

"Probably a hunting camp. Game must always have come to water near the creek."

"Oh, look, here's another," she said, raising an arrowhead close to Kincaid's eyes, as if he were as nearsighted as she was. "Uncle will be pleased. He's awfully eager to find artifacts."

"For the Rutledge Museum?"

"You know about that, and Lord Bertram? It's awfully important to Uncle that he not be upstaged by Lord Bertram. He's a terrible, howling old fool."

"Your uncle?"

"Lord Bertram, of course," she answered without a hint of a smile. "Oh, there's Benjamin now."

Kincaid glanced that way. "It's only Farnsworth," he told her. How bad were her eyes?

"Oh. Well, I expect he's napping, then. This is a terrible jaunt for Benjie and myself. Though perhaps not so bad for Benjie, who does like to shoot. For myself it's been only excessive heat and a lot of jolting around across rough country. A terrible bore."

"Why did you come?" Kincaid asked as they began walking back toward camp.

"Oh, well. Uncle insisted I come—he's my guardian, you see—and Benjie, of course, couldn't stay behind. We're to be married as soon as we return to England, though the way this expedition has gone, that will be simply ages."

"It always seems like ages to two people in love," Kincaid said diplomatically.

"Yes, I expect you're right. Goodbye and thank you, Lieutenant." She took his hand and gave it a dry, proper shake.

Kincaid noticed Benjamin Doyle standing in the shade cast by the tent, and he hoped Suzanne could see well enough to find him. Grinning, Matt turned away and walked up to the army camp, where Corson, Holzer, and Rafferty were cleaning up after dinner.

"Seen Sergeant Cohen?"

"No, sir," Rafferty answered.

"To bath in the local river water," Holzer said helpfully.

"I see." Kincaid smiled faintly.

"Sir, are we going to remain in this camp for long?" Rafferty asked. "We haven't pitched our tents. Didn't seem much point in it. Now it looks like the earl is going to stay around. Any information?"

"Nothing's been said to me. I'll ask, though." Kincaid glanced at Fremont, who, to Kincaid's surprise, stood glowering back at him. *What's the matter with him now?* Kincaid wondered.

Fremont just hadn't fit in. He seemed to go out of his way to find trouble. Cohen had reported the scuffle with Malone, as well as the problem between Pettigrew and Fremont.

A moment later, Kincaid had other things to think

about. Rafferty lifted an arm, and Kincaid turned to see the dark mass of the buffalo herd ambling toward them. They had come back, driven by Whitechapel's men, who encouraged them along.

They hadn't come back alone. Off along the creek, Kincaid saw the Cheyenne hunting party eyeing the herd, the drovers, and the tents of Lord Whitechapel.

"Throw your saddles up, men. This could mean anything."

Rafferty was already doing just that, although he had gone for his rifle first and his saddle second. Ben Cohen was charging back up from the creek, shirtless, hat in hand.

"Get Pettigrew and Malone," Kincaid ordered Corson, and the enlisted man set off at a run.

"You saw them?" Ben Cohen panted, belting his pistol on.

"Just now."

"What do you want to do?"

"Nothing, Ben. They're hostiles, I expect, but damn it, we can't open up a shooting war with the civilians here. How many do you make out?"

"Ten, fifteen."

"That we can see."

"That's it, sir."

Malone and Pettigrew were coming on the double, and now Kincaid saw His Lordship himself step out into the glare of sunlight, peering toward Kincaid.

Matt headed that way and found Lord Whitechapel waiting impatiently, tugging at his mustache.

"What in blazes is going on, Kincaid? People scurrying all around, scaring the wits out of my staff."

"There, sir," Kincaid said, gently directing the earl's attention to the mounted warriors across the creek.

"Is that all? A few blasted natives! Kincaid, you astonish me. But, by Jove! The beaters have driven the herd back. Farnsworth! Farnsworth! Bring my guns."

With that, Whitechapel turned and strode toward the knoll. Ben Cohen, rushing up afoot, asked breathlessly, "What's happening?"

"Nothing much, Ben," Matt sighed, and rubbed his neck. "His Lordship has seen the Cheyenne and decided to start shooting."

nine

    His Lordship, followed by his gunbearer, was walking to the low knoll where he had done his shooting earlier in the day. Across the creek sat fifteen armed, hostile Cheyenne Indians, who had probably come to hunt the same buffalo herd, only to find a strange assortment of white men camped on their hunting grounds.

    "Lord Whitechapel!" Kincaid had corraled the earl again, and now he said, "I ask you not to start firing. It might very well be misinterpreted by the Indians. You are already hunting their buffalo. I'm afraid they might take this to heart."

    "Nonsense," Whitechapel replied gruffly. "Farnsworth, the Rigby. Lieutenant, are you going to stand aside?"

    There wasn't a whole lot of choice. What was he going to do otherwise, wrestle the lord to the ground? "Sir," he tried again in desperation, "I beg you to consider this carefully. They may retaliate."

"Well, then, sir, that is what we have soldiers along for, isn't it? Cartridges, Farnsworth."

Kincaid turned away before he could say what was on his mind. Cohen read the expression quickly.

"Going to have his hunt anyway, is he?"

Kincaid didn't take time to answer. "Mount the men and post them in plain sight, Ben. Over there, I think. Let's at least give them second thoughts, although I don't suppose it will do us much good if they get themselves worked up over this."

Cohen hadn't yet issued the order when the huge. 480 Rigby roared, and a buffalo a hundred yards off sagged to its knees and died.

Kincaid saw the Cheyenne turn their horses and start to ride for cover, several of them dropping down below the shoulders of their ponies before they realized the rifle fire was not being directed at them.

They whirled, and it was at that moment that Kincaid thought they would charge.

Instead they halted again at the creek and sat watching. Lord Whitechapel continued to fire, and Doyle had now joined in. The buffalo were dropping one by one, the guns roaring like dry thunder.

"What are they going to do?" Malone was looking at the Cheyenne, seeing the impatience in them. Their horses sidestepped nervously. The guns fired.

Pettigrew had started shaking, but he didn't know why. He had fought before on numerous occasions. Perhaps it was because he had so little time left to serve in the army, perhaps because he now had something to live for.

Finally Lord Whitechapel put his gun aside, and after another two rounds had been fired by Doyle, the shooting was ended. Thirty buffalo lay dead on the grass.

His Lordship turned to Kincaid. "Now let's have a talk with the natives, shall we?"

"A talk? Sir, that is utterly inadvisable."

"Why? Make friends with them wherever possible, I always say. Come, Kincaid, I know you're a soldier, but let's make powwow."

Kincaid shook his head slowly, the weight of the world on his shoulders. This man was determined to get himself killed. And if that happened, Kincaid would be held accountable, no two ways about it.

"Come, Doyle," Whitechapel said. "I'm riding down to speak to them."

Doyle didn't look too anxious to go along. Matt, not seeing much choice, muttered, "Wait, I'll come with you. Rafferty!"

"Sir!"

"How's your sign lingo?"

"All right," Rafferty shrugged. It was better than most white men's, and Rafferty cursed the day he had let the army know that. He had acted as translator in some ticklish situations, and now was up again.

"The three of us, then. Don't want them to think it's a war party."

"Kincaid! Are you coming or not?"

"Coming, sir." Kincaid bit off the rest of his remarks. He mounted his bay and fell in behind Lord Whitechapel. Doyle wisely elected to stay behind. Rafferty shot his lieutenant a nervous glance. They rode slowly across the grass, the scent of gunpowder still lingering as the remainder of the buffalo herd wandered southward, still not knowing what had happened.

"Stupid animals," Lord Whitechapel observed accurately.

Now Kincaid could see the unpainted faces of the

Cheyenne. There were an even dozen of them, all poorly armed. Most had bows and arrows. There were two muzzle-loaders and one ancient Hawken.

Kincaid, with no feeling of security, raised a hand, and when there was no response they rode ahead across the creek, Lord Whitechapel chattering a mile a minute.

"I say, fine-looking specimens, aren't they? Look at the chest on that fellow. Cheyenne, are they? Ask them where their camp is. I'd love to see how they live. Might take the whole bloody bunch of them back with me. Let 'em camp in the Rutledge. That would give Bertram a proper pain."

They halted their horses, facing the Cheyenne, whose bronzed faces were expressionless. They held their weapons and stared in turn at Lord Whitechapel, at the dead buffalo, at Kincaid.

"Tell them this, Rafferty: This man is a great hunter from across the sea, the big water, however you sign that. He has come to see the land of the Cheyenne, to see how they live, to see the buffalo, since his land is poor in game."

Rafferty was having a little trouble. He must have gotten crossed up once or twice, since they stared at his hands with puzzlement. They seemed to get the gist of it, however.

"Tell them that all the meat is for them," Lord Whitechapel put in. "Tell them it is a gift from me."

Rafferty did so with growing uneasiness. The Cheyenne simply sat their ponies, looking at the three white men. Finally the oldest man there, the one with four feathers knotted into his glossy hair, answered in sign language, and Kincaid watched Rafferty anxiously.

"Well?"

"They said—" Rafferty hesitated, frowning as if he couldn't believe what he thought they said. "They said that he is indeed a great hunter. They have never seen such a fine shot. They thank him for the meat. Their village is hungry and their weapons are poor."

"That's all?" Kincaid asked.

"Of course that's all, Kincaid," Lord Whitechapel said, looking down his nose at the Cheyenne. "Tell the native leader that I am gratifed by his compliments, a compliment which means much, coming from the greatest hunting men in the world. Tell them that there will be much more meat if they wish to follow along after my party. Tell them they are welcome to it all."

At Rafferty's translation, the leader of the Cheyenne actually broke into a smile. He answered rapidly and Rafferty said, "He thinks that's a fine idea, sir. Says he appreciates the great hunter's generosity."

"God," Kincaid said under his breath. "Sir, with all respect, I can't believe it's a good idea to have these Indians traveling along behind us. You never know what notion's liable to pop into their skulls."

"Nonsense. I made the offer. My word is my bond." He waved a hand and told Rafferty, "Tell them they are my friends. I promise them much meat."

Then he turned and rode off, splashing across the stream, his big black horse throwing up tiny spurs of silver water. Rafferty looked at Kincaid.

"Tell them, Private. Tell them they are guests of the great hunter."

Rafferty, swallowing hard, did so. Then, cautiously, the two soldiers retreated across the river, riding to the knoll where the rest of the Easy Company men sat watching.

"Well?" Cohen asked excitedly.

"The natives will be joining the safari," Kincaid said tonelessly

As Kincaid watched, the Cheyenne women began to

emerge from the coulees. Escorted by the men, they went out onto the plain and began skinning the buffalo. Lord Whitechapel, like some feudal benefactor, sat watching "his" natives at their work before, yawning, he announced himself ready for luncheon.

They drifted southward toward the Medicine Bow Mountains, His Lordship's appetite for bear and cougar trophies drawing them into the foothills.

Already they saw occasional scattered timber, spruce and cedar, although the country was mostly flat, rolling toward the south.

Whitechapel downed three elk out of one herd, an amazing feat. Elk, unlike the stolid buffalo, were jolted into motion by the scent of trouble. The bull elk, trophy size, was dropped as he stood grazing, but the second and third were taken on the run, at long range.

Whitechapel took the head of the big bull and left the rest for the Cheyenne.

"They're still back there," Malone grumbled to Corson.

"I know. Caught sight of a couple not an hour ago."

"Man's crazy," Malone commented.

"They're just skinning the game," Pettigrew said, "taking the meat back to their camp. Why not? His Lordship's only leaving it to rot."

Malone shifted in his saddle, yawning prodigiously. "I just don't like it. It ain't natural to have a band of hostiles following you around. Next thing to be skinned is us."

"Pettigrew don't think the Indians would do a nasty thing like that, do you, Petty?" Fremont asked tauntingly.

"I've seen more Indian fighting than you ever will," Andy answered sharply.

"And more Indian *lovin'*."

92

"Dammit, Fremont! I'm not about to take a whole lot more of your shit!"

"Did I hurt your feelings?" Fremont leaned out of the saddle, a simpering, mocking expression on his face, and Pettigrew lifted a boot out of the stirrup and kicked him squarely in the face.

Fremont's horse bucked and Fremont fell free, landing flat on his back, blood spewing from his nose. Holzer had to rein in hard to avoid trampling the soldier.

Before anyone could react, Pettigrew had leaped from the saddle, landing on Fremont's chest and belly with his knees. The big man groaned and started to gag. Pettigrew slammed his fist into Fremont's face, hearing gristle give. It should have torn his head off, but it didn't.

Fremont was a big man, and a strong one. He roared with anger and pain, threw Pettigrew aside, and came to his knees, his pistol in hand.

"Fire that thing and I'll kill you, Fremont, so help me God!" The voice was Ben Cohen's. The first shirt had come riding up on the double. Now he sat, his Springfield rifle to his shoulder, looking down the sights at Fremont, who hesitated a long moment before finally nodding and holstering his gun.

He remained kneeling in the dust, blood trickling from his mouth and nose.

Cohen had dismounted and he now walked to Fremont, lifting him to his feet by his shirtfront. "Come here!" Ben roared at Pettigrew, and the soldier shuffled hesitantly toward Cohen, who pushed Fremont away and stood glaring at both soldiers.

"This is how it is. There's not going to be any more of this crap! Not a word, not a look. If there is, I'm sending the man responsible off walking back toward Number Nine. Alone. Afoot. Maybe he'll make it back to report to Captain Conway, maybe the Cheyenne will get him. I don't know which would be worse. But I'll stand for no more of it!"

Cohen swung back onto his bay's back and rode off. Malone whistled softly. "That was his dead serious face, boys. What he said was exactly what he meant. I'd lie low, was I you." He winked before starting his horse. "Take it from a man who knows."

It was early the following morning, in the very shadow of the Medicine Bows, that William Stonebrook found cougar tracks along a stream that trickled down through the foothills.

Whitechapel was in what was, for him, a frenzy of excitement. That is to say, he lifted one eyebrow higher than the other.

"Trophy size, Stonebrook?"

"I should say so, sir. Has paws like an elephant."

"Where?"

"Along the stream," Stonebrook said, pointing. "I followed the tracks up into those hills." Where Stonebrook pointed, a series of pale sandstone bluffs rose toward the higher foothills. Here and there, gnarled, wind-torn cedars clung tenuously to the poor soil. Higher up grew a small stand of spruce.

"Quite a climb."

"Yes, sir, but I imagine he comes down to the creek each night to drink. Probably follows pretty much the same course each time."

"Let's have a look at those tracks. Kincaid! Come along and tell me what you think."

Kincaid obeyed the royal command. They went afoot along the quick-running, crystal-clear creek, toward the sandstone bluffs where Stonebrook had seen the mountain lion tracks.

Lord Whitechapel went unarmed, Kincaid carrying

only his Schofield pistol. Stonebrook led the way up-creek, fighting through the dry willows that clotted a section of the streambed.

"Here we are," Stonebrook said. He crouched, flashing his gap-toothed smile. Kincaid bent over his shoulder to study the tracks imprinted in the soft, sandy soil.

"Well?" Whitechapel asked.

"It's a big one, sir," Kincaid answered. "Not much doubt about that."

"How big?"

"Couldn't say exactly." If Windy had been there, he probably could have judged from the length of the cat's stride. But Windy wasn't there—he was lucky. "Big enough," Matt concluded.

Stonebrook rose, clapping the dust from his hands. "He'll likely return this evening to water, sir. We can improve our chances by staking some bait. A nice buffalo haunch, maybe."

"Sundown, you think?" Whitechapel asked, looking up along the layered bluffs.

"I would think so, sir."

"Very well, we'll have at him."

"Lord Whitechapel," Kincaid put in, "I don't know if you've hunted cougar before—"

"Took twenty lion one winter in Kenya," Whitechapel said.

"There is some difference between an African lion and a cougar," Kincaid said. "First of all, the mountain lion's a climbing beast. He's liable to place himself above you, especially since we've pretty well left our scent around the area."

"Kincaid," Whitechapel said in his driest voice. "I can assure you that I am a gamesman. I've done a deal of shooting, I daresay more than you will do in a lifetime. There is, of course, an element of danger when dealing with the big cats, but that only serves to make the hunt twenty times more interesting than shooting buffalo or elk."

The matter was closed. Lord Whitechapel spun and walked briskly away, leaving Kincaid to stare at the tracks of a massive and very dangerous cougar.

The Cheyenne were in the camp when Kincaid and Whitechapel returned.

They were men, one of them in a ceremonial bonnet. They stood beside their horses in front of Whitechapel's tent, arms folded, eyes stony.

"Welcome, welcome," Whitechapel said. He walked directly to them, then circled them slowly, studying their dress. Kincaid stood back at a little distance, looking not only at the Cheyenne warriors he could see, but scanning the hills and riverbottom for those he could not.

"Now then, Kincaid, send for that interpreter of yours, will you?"

"I speak," the tallest of the Cheyenne said.

"English! How splendid." Whitechapel was obviously not about to invite the natives inside, but he asked if they would like food and drink.

When they answered affirmatively, Whitechapel said, "Farnsworth, bring these gentlemen food and wine." Kincaid started to object, but Whitechapel, obviously somewhat annoyed, said, "Really, Kincaid, you've done nothing but interfere. I don't wonder that the army's had trouble on the plains. A little friendliness can go a long way. Is it the wine? Really, a man can't be expected to have a meal without a little wine. It's not liquor."

He turned back to the tall Cheyenne, who was a smug-looking man with shifty eyes. "Now then, sir, what can I do for you?"

"Trade."

"Trade? My dear sir, I am not a trader. In fact, I have

96

little that I expect you would find use for."

"Guns," the Cheyenne said.

"My weapons!" Whitechapel approached open laughter. "I doubt, sir, that there is anything in all your magnificent land for which I would trade my weapons. Ah, here's the pheasant and wine. Please be seated and eat. Farnsworth, have one of the girls bring a rug for these gentlemen to sit on. Pardon me, sir, I didn't catch your name."

"Name Twelve Sky."

"Yes, Mr. Twelve Sky. Whitechapel's mine. Here's the girl with the rug. Please be seated, have something to eat if you will."

The Indians did so, still wary and ill at ease. They poked at the pheasant, finally tasted it and, finding it palatable, tore it to pieces with their fingers, eating with obvious enjoyment. The wine went over even better.

"Now then, Mr. Twelve Sky," Whitechapel said when they were nearly finished, "I am, as you may have guessed, interested in Indian artifacts. Your war bonnet, for instance, would make an intriguing addition to my collection. I would be happy to let you have a horse for that."

"No horse. Guns."

"Impossible, old man. Would you like to look at them?"

"Yes. Let me see guns."

At Whitechapel's command, the gun cases were brought out and placed on the blanket before the Cheyenne. To a man who owned only a Civil War muzzle-loader and who had never imagined anything more superb than a Winchester repeater, the guns of his lordship must have seemed incredible, a gift from the gods.

Twelve Sky's eyes were the size of saucers. He let his finger follow the gold filigree work on the receiver of the Rigby, stroking the polished stock of the rifle, which lay cushioned in red velvet.

"I will have," Twelve Sky said abruptly.

"Sorry, old man, you definitely will *not* have."

"Ten ponies."

"No. I have many horses."

"Ten ponies. This." He removed his war bonnet and gestured.

"Not enough, I'm afraid, Mr. Twelve Sky. I want nothing badly enough to part with that weapon."

Twelve Sky stood, and Matt Kincaid let his hand rest on the butt of his holstered Scoff. "You will give me guns."

"No, I won't," Whitechapel said calmly. If the Cheyenne had thought to intimidate Whitechapel, he had met his match. The earl was unshakable.

"Two wives," Twelve Sky said, leering. "I will trade two wives."

"Sorry, Mr. Twelve Sky. I already have all the English law allows."

It was then that Virginia Whitechapel came up to stand beside her husband, her blue eyes sparkling with amusement, and Twelve Sky, looking at this white woman, knew that the Englishman had no need for another wife.

"Now, gentlemen, if you will excuse me, it is time for me to think about a bath."

Farnsworth was closing the gun cases and Twelve Sky's eyes were riveted to them, looking away only after they were picked up and transported back into the massive striped tent.

"I will have guns," the Cheyenne said again.

"Yes, well, I'm afraid we can't trade, Mr. Twelve Sky. I hope you've enjoyed your meal. Do come back again sometime." With that, Whitechapel turned and swept into the tent.

The Cheyenne stood for a moment longer, then Twelve

Sky snatched up his war bonnet and leaped onto his pony's back. Followed by the others, he raced from the camp, whooping and shouting.

When the dust had settled, Virginia walked to where Kincaid stood watching.

"Trouble?" she asked, her breast brushing his arm.

"I don't know. A good rifle means a lot to these people. In a culture where you live by the hunt, weapons are indicative of a man's worth. Twelve Sky wants those weapons. How much he wants them is anyone's guess."

"Then you believe he might attempt to steal them?"

"I couldn't say."

"Lieutenant?" She glanced once toward the tent and then turned to him again, her fingers toying with the buttons on his tunic. "Why do you ignore me? It's really most impolite of you."

"I wasn't aware that I had been ignoring you."

"No?" Lady Whitechapel suppressed a smile. "Why, you've even gone out walking with Suzanne in the evening. Is it that you prefer little Suzanne to me?"

"The fact is, Lady Whitechapel, that you are a married woman," Kincaid said a little stiffly.

"Your career."

"Pardon me?"

"I see now, it is your career you are worried about. My husband's influence."

"Frankly, that is a part of it."

"But you do not find me unattractive?" she asked, her eyelashes batting furiously as she clutched her breast.

"I assure you, my perceptions are quite to the contrary," Kincaid answered, bowing slightly and touching the brim of his hat, then walking away.

"Then," she said, her voice following him, "we shall simply have to find a way to avoid discovery, because Lieutenant Kincaid, I find you entirely irresistible."

"Trouble, sir?" Cohen asked.

"What?" Kincaid looked up in confusion.

"The Cheyenne."

Kincaid had to smile. He had completely forgotten the Indians in the last five minutes. "No, Ben. No trouble," he answered. Then, looking back toward the camp, where Virginia still stood watching, he added, "Damn the woman!"

ten _____

"Coming along, I assume, Kincaid?"

"Yes, I'm coming." Matt looked toward the western skies, where the sun was slowly sinking into the dark horizon. The thin, high clouds were gilded, the shadows at the foot of the mountains bleeding out onto the plains.

Matt had his Springfield with him. They were going after cougar.

Whitechapel, when he arrived, was flushed with excitement, eager to be at the "big cat," as he called it. Matt wasn't so sure about the wisdom of this. Going into the cougar's home ground at this time of the evening could be foolhardy. Matt's only reason for going was that he might provide some additional protection for Whitechapel. Matt had seen stalking cougars before, and he didn't like them. Quick, shadowy, powerful, they were best left alone, in Kincaid's opinion.

"He's mine, Kincaid," Lord Whitechapel said, noticing that Matt had a rifle with him.

"He's all yours, sir. Don't know what I'd do with a trophy head anyway."

"Quite. Lead off, Stonebrook."

The sky still held a bluish-gold tint as they worked upstream toward the thickly shadowed hills, but it would be dark soon enough.

They pushed through the willow brush as silently as possible, and then, with hand gestures, Stonebrook guided them to a ledge he had spotted earlier in the day. From there the bait left for the prowling cougar should be visible, and from there, if Whitechapel's luck was running true, he should have a good shot at his big cat.

They crawled up onto the ledge, which still held the heat of the day, Matt going to his belly beside the earl. The wind drifted downriver, carrying their scent away from any approaching animal. The shadows collected in deep pools now, and the sky held only a vaguely reddish glow. Matt found himself hoping they didn't run into the cougar that night.

He came suddenly alert. Something had moved down along the river, and Matt touched Whitechapel's arm. A moment later they saw what it was.

A four-point mule deer buck crept from the brush to the water's edge and lowered his muzzle to drink.

Abruptly the deer's head went up, and in three bounds he was gone, across the stream and into the brush. Matt shifted uneasily. The deer hadn't caught their scent. What scent, then, *had* it detected?

He strained his eyes against the night, searching the riverbed inch by inch, looking for a creature that would make no sound at all as it traveled. The bait, a raw buffalo haunch, lay untouched next to the creek. It was rapidly growing too dark for decent shooting.

It came with a purr of sound and a whisper of movement, a leaping shadow. Kincaid rolled onto his back, realizing too late that the cougar had been on the ledge above them, watching.

Matt tried to bring his Springfield up, and failed. The cougar collided with his body, smelling musty, its fierce, muscular body sprawled across his.

Only then did he hear the echo of the shot Lord Whitechapel had fired as the cat leaped. Kincaid lay beneath the mountain lion, looking up into its slavering mouth. With disgust and awe he shoved the giant cat from him, feeling the warm blood trickling down his wrist and arm.

He stood unsteadily to find Whitechapel calmly watching him.

"Close one, eh?"

"Too close."

"Big cat."

"Yes." Kincaid had recovered himself. "Thank you, sir. One swipe of that paw, and there wouldn't have been much left of me."

"Nonsense. No thanks necessary. I put you into this spot, didn't I? My responsibility, you know. You would have done the same for me, Kincaid."

"Thanks anyway," Matt said, picking up his hat and rifle. Stonebrook was crouched over the cougar.

"This isn't the one," he said.

"What's that?"

"Wrong cat. Look, three toes on the hind foot. It's a female, possibly the big one's mate."

Whitechapel looked disappointed, but said nothing. Matt shook his head. This man was something else. Cool, haughty, obstinate, generous, inflexible. And a hell of a shot. He had picked that leaping cougar out of the air in poor light, his reflexes as quick as a fencer's.

"Had enough?" Whitechapel asked, and there seemed to be real concern in his voice.

"I've had enough for tonight," Matt wasn't ashamed to admit. "Going back?"

"After a minute. I'll wait for Stonebrook to skin this one out." Whitechapel placed a hand briefly on Matt's shoulder. "Go on in and wash up. Have yourself a drink."

"I believe I will." The cougar blood was smeared across his tunic, the scent of it heavy in his nostrils. He clambered down off the ledge, feeling more shaky than he would have admitted to anyone.

Walking through the willow brush, temporarily silencing the frogs that grumbled there, Matt came to the creek. He took off his tunic and threw it aside. Kneeling, he washed his face, hands, and chest. Then he threw his head back and looked up to the starry skies, taking a deep, slow breath.

He rose and turned away, and the woman rushed into his arms.

The lips found his, the arms encircled his waist. She was close against him, whispering passionately.

"Oh, Benjie. Benjie, take me!"

"Miss Ridgeley."

"Oh, God!" she shrieked and fell away, her hands going to her mouth. "In the darkness . . . my eyes . . ." she stammered.

"It's all right. Don't worry about it."

"My God, I thought—"

"God damn you, you bastard!" the voice roared out of the night. "Kincaid! I knew it. The way you've been cozying up to Suzanne, taking her for evening walks."

"No, Benjie!" Suzanne Ridgeley gasped. "I was coming to meet you, as I promised. It's my eyes. I can't see a thing in the darkness. There's nothing between Lieutenant Kincaid and me."

"I don't believe it. *I* have good eyes, and I have seen

enough. You have not heard the last of this, Kincaid, I promise you!"

With that, Benjamin Doyle stalked off into the night shadows, Suzanne Ridgeley stumbling after him, whimpering and pleading.

Kincaid picked up his tunic and stood sullenly in the darkness for a minute. "I have definitely had enough," he thought. Then he shook his head and crossed the creek, heading for the Easy Company camp and sanity.

Nearing Whitechapel's tent, he thought he heard some giggling in the long grass, and he paused, frowning. After a minute there was a low voice that sounded for all the world like Malone's. It shouldn't have been Malone. He was supposedly down in the scullery, washing pots. Maybe it was two servants, having a roll in the grass.

Whoever it was, Kincaid had no wish at all to walk into another unfortunate situation, and he stumped on toward his tent, putting it out of his mind.

"Quiet night, sir, real nice."

Ben Cohen was sitting by the campfire, which was now only softly glowing coals, looking up at the starry sky.

"Very nice," Kincaid muttered. Then he went into his tent and lay down to sleep, thinking of the peaceful life he had once led, interrupted only by Indian wars and outlaws.

He was roused an hour before dawn, and he rolled out ready to chew Cohen up for waking him so early. But it wasn't Ben Cohen at the tent flap.

It was Farnsworth, in frock coat and top hat. Kincaid blinked at this apparition. The stout man was utterly serious.

"With Mr. Doyle's compliments."

"What?"

105

Farnsworth handed Kincaid an engraved card. He turned it over, but there was nothing on it other than Doyle's name.

"What is this?"

"Sir, Mr. Doyle hereby challenges you."

"Challenges me?"

"To a duel, sir."

"A duel!" Kincaid laughed out loud, deepening Farnsworth's frown. "What in hell for?"

"For reasons best known to you and Mr. Doyle, I assume, sir. I believe it involves your trifling with Miss Ridgeley's affections, but then you certainly know more than I pretend to about the particulars."

"Actually, Farnsworth, I know less than you do about Mr. Doyle's motives. There is nothing at all going on. This is all a gross mistake. I refuse to duel the man. You may take him my answer." With that, Kincaid tore up the card and dropped it to the floor of his tent.

"Very good, sir," Farnsworth said, bowing out. Kincaid was left to stare after him.

"Everything all right, sir?" Ben Cohen asked, peering into the tent sleepily.

"Couldn't be better."

Cohen shrugged, studying Matt's face for a minute. "We've got something up out here. The Cheyenne are back."

Closing his eyes tightly, taking a deep breath, Matt nodded slowly and began dressing. Minutes later he went out to find three Cheyenne ponies drawn up before Lord Whitechapel's tent. Dawn was just lighting the eastern skies with orange and subtle crimson. Kincaid walked down the slope, glancing toward the aloof Medicine Bows beyond the foothills.

He heard Whitechapel's voice long before he got to the tent. "No, no. Sorry, my friend. Can't be done."

Spread on the ground before Whitechapel's tent was an

array of blankets, headdresses, beaded garments, neck-laces, ceramic pots, silver conchos—and holding up each article in turn was Twelve Sky.

"Listen, I'd be happy to buy these articles from you," the earl said. "I'd give you a fair price in gold or horses. But my weapons, sir, are not up for barter."

"Guns," Twelve Sky said, showing Whitechapel a striped blanket. Whitechapel just shook his head.

"No. Sorry, old fellow. If you want to sell these arti-facts, I'll be happy to purchase them. The Rutledge would be pleased to have this collection, I daresay, but I cannot trade my guns."

"Everything all right?" Kincaid asked.

"Oh, Kincaid. Feeling all right this morning? No trou-ble. This gentleman has simply returned to try to barter me out of my rifles. I've been trying to explain to him that all he has is not worth so much to me as my Rigby."

"No trade," Kincaid said, and Twelve Sky looked at him coldly.

Abruptly, Twelve Sky spun away, his face reflecting anger. He said something to his two assistants and they collected the trade goods. They silently mounted their ponies, silently rode away, Twelve Sky's face still angry.

"He's hungry for that rifle," Matt said. "You'll have to watch your weapons. They have been known to lift an item or two."

"Oh, I think he understands now, Kincaid. It seems to me—"

Lord Whitechapel was interrupted by the man in the powder-blue suit who rushed past his lordship to smash his fist into Kincaid's mouth.

Matt's head spun around. Warm blood filled his mouth. He started reflexively to fight back, realized that it would be a mistake, and stood staring at Benjamin Doyle, who was shaking with emotion. The young blond man had

107

worked himself into a fever. His fists were balled, his jaw set belligerently.

"Here, here!" Lord Whitechapel boomed. "What is all this?"

"A matter of honor," Doyle panted. "This man is a coward and a trifler. I have challenged him and he hasn't the manhood to accept."

Kincaid felt his hackles slowly rising, felt his blood begin to boil. He tried to calm himself, but it wasn't working well.

"A matter of honor?" Whitechapel said, his eyebrows drawing together. "I am sure you are mistaken, Doyle."

"I am not." In the background somewhere, Suzanne Ridgeley was whimpering again. Kincaid caught a glimpse of Virginia, appearing cool and amused, standing beside the tent.

"I am not mistaken," Doyle said again, emphatically. "And I am naming this American a coward and a blackguard. I demand satisfaction."

Matt stood staring at the excited young Englishman, who looked foolish in his pale blue coat, which had slipped off one shoulder. Doyle's face was crimson with excitement, and Matt heard his own voice, as if it came from someone else far distant, say finally, "I accept your challenge."

eleven _____

Lord Whitechapel sucked in his breath. Matt saw Virginia's hand fly up to her mouth as Suzanne, beside her, gasped and swayed slightly as if she were about to faint. Lady Whitechapel put an arm around the smaller woman to steady her. Doyle's face, which had been purple and apoplectic-looking, suddenly drained of all color, as though the lethal reality of the situation had just struck him—as indeed, perhaps, it had.

"As the challenged, the choice of weapons is y-yours, sir," Doyle stammered, attempting to square his normally sloping shoulders.

"I realize that, sir," Kincaid replied. "Unfortunately, as an officer in the United States Army, I am forbidden by regulations to engage in a duel involving the use of weapons."

Doyle bristled. "How, then, sir, is honor to be satisfied?"

Kincaid smiled graciously. "When I was a cadet at West Point," he began, "we used to settle disputes in a formally arranged, refereed boxing match. I suggest we use the same method here."

"Fisticuffs?" Doyle said distastefully. "It hardly seems to me that a gentleman—"

"Nonsense," Lord Whitechapel interrupted. "It seems a capital idea to me. Can't imagine what this is all about, of course, but such a bout might provide us all with a bit of jolly good diversion."

"But—" Doyle started to protest.

"Now, now, bad form, Benjamin," the earl cut in. "After all, you were the one to extend the challenge. It is certainly Lieutenant Kincaid's right to choose the weapons."

"I suppose," Doyle said, clearly disgruntled. He was sizing Kincaid up. The two men were about equal in height, but Kincaid was tanned and sinewy, whereas Doyle was pale, and his only exercise recently had consisted of lifting a rifle to his shoulder. The tic began again in the corner of the Englishman's eye as he said, "Very well, sir, fisticuffs it is. Choose your second."

A square area of ground had been cleared of grass and stamped smooth near a stand of box elders just outside the camp. Members of Lord Whitechapel's retinue, as well as the entire Easy Company contingent, were crowded around, waiting in growing excitement for the contest to get under way.

Matt Kincaid and his opponent sat on stools at opposite corners of the makeshift ring, both stripped to the waist. Doyle, his bare torso pallid and lacking definition in the morning sunlight, looked morose as he nodded occasionally in response to the whispered advice of his second, Farnsworth, who hovered over him, kneading his shoulders vigorously.

110

From the beginning, there had been no doubt as to who Kincaid's second would be. Ben Cohen squatted next to the lieutenant, shaking his head as he sized up the two contenders. "Bad situation, sir," he said. "That fellow over there looks as though if you breathed on him hard, he'd evaporate. This whole thing could be over damn quick. The tough part is, we're not supposed to let anything happen to any of these folks, otherwise we'll have the State Department and War all over us. But if you refuse to fight that pup, it'll make us all look bad."

"It's ticklish, all right," Matt agreed.

"Well, how the hell do you figure to handle it, sir?" Cohen asked.

Matt reached out a hand and clapped the first sergeant on the shoulder. "Diplomacy, Ben, diplomacy."

Matt surveyed the crowd around the ring. The soldiers were all gathered around his corner; now and then one of them would lean forward and speak a word of encouragement. Across the ring, Virginia Whitechapel and Suzanne Doyle stood together. Suzanne still looked as if she might faint at any moment, but Virginia had recovered her composure, and was gazing openly at Matt's tanned, bare chest and taut stomach above the waist of his blue trousers. Their eyes met, and she allowed a ghost of a smile to flicker at the corner of her mouth before she glanced away.

Lord Whitechapel himself had volunteered to act as referee, and now there was a ripple of excitement among the spectators as the earl made his way through them and stepped to the center of the cleared area. Conversation ceased as he raised his hands for silence.

"Ladies and gentlemen," he began, "we are assembled here to witness the settling of an affair of honor between two gentlemen. Benjamin Doyle of the Whitechapel expedition, and Lieutenant Kincaid of the United States

Army. The rules of the match will be those set down for the practice of fisticuffs by the Marquis of Queensberry. Only the use of fists will be allowed, the winner of the bout to be determined by his opponent's failure to rise before a count of ten. Any call for quarter will be adjudged an admission of defeat. The bout will last ten rounds of three minutes' duration each. If there is no clear winner at the end of ten rounds, the fight will be declared a draw. The beginning and end of each round will be announced by a blast upon this whistle." He displayed a brass whistle hung around his neck from a leather thong. "Ready, gentlemen?" The opponents nodded. "Jolly good! Let the contest begin, and may the best man win!" He raised the whistle to his lips, sounded a strident blast on it, and stepped gingerly to a neutral corner.

The voices of the spectators rose quickly to an excited murmur as the opponents rose from their stools and warily approached the center of the ring. They began to circle each other. Doyle was hunched over, his fists describing circles in front of his face. Kincaid stood loosely, arms and shoulders relaxed, his fists in front of his chest. Doyle began to duck and dodge from side to side, although not a single punch had yet been thrown. Finally he made a tentative jab with his left, which Kincaid easily blocked with his right forearm. He jabbed again, and Kincaid blocked that punch with equal ease.

"Come on, sir, make it short and sweet!" Malone's voice yelled from the sidelines, and was instantly supported by the affirming cries of the rest of the soldiers.

Doyle continued to toss punches, a flurry of them now, and Kincaid continued to block them effortlessly. And so it went for the remainder of the first round, until Lord Whitechapel blew his whistle and the opponents returned to their corners.

Doyle's chest was heaving from his exertions, and

Farnsworth dried his perspiring shoulders with a towel and then gave him a drink of water from a bottle.

Ben Cohen looked disgusted as Matt sat calmly on his stool, a thoughtful expression on his face. "Christ, sir," Cohen said, "why don't you just finish him off?"

Matt smiled at him and said only one word: "Diplomacy."

Lord Whitechapel blew his whistle, signaling the beginning of the second round, and the contenders again approached each other. The second round was much like the first, and at its conclusion the two men retired to their corners, Doyle's pale torso now sporting a definite crimson flush, perspiration streaming from his scalp. Cohen looked even more disgusted, and the rest of the soldiers had fallen silent, wondering what the hell was going on.

The third round began with a blast of the whistle, and started out like the previous two. But toward the end of the round, in the midst of one volley of punches, Kincaid tossed an abrupt right at Doyle's chest. It connected, feeling to Kincaid as if he were punching a pillow, and Doyle let out a *whoof!* and staggered backwards a step or two. The army contingent cheered, and a gasp went up from the Whitechapel party. Doyle's face was set in a determined grimace as he closed in again and Matt launched another right with the same results as before. Suzanne buried her face in Virginia's shoulder, and the whistle sounded the end of the third round.

When Doyle collapsed on his stool, Suzanne rushed to him, holding his hand as he panted for breath, whispering encouragement to him as he stared up at the sky.

"Sir, for God's sake, this is plain silly!" Cohen said to Kincaid.

"Don't worry, Ben," Kincaid said calmly. "I think this next round will be the last one."

"Thank the Lord you're finally going to finish him off, sir," Malone put in. "I don't think the lad can stand much more without just fainting away."

The fourth round began, and Doyle nearly staggered out of his corner. Matt just waited for him at the center of the ring, and when Doyle stepped within range, Kincaid threw two light, rapid jabs that took Doyle on the nose. The Englishman's head jerked back and he backstepped a pace or two, blood pouring from his nose. He reached a hand up to his face and then took it away, looking at his bloodstained fingers. Then he looked up at Kincaid, grimacing in rage.

"By God, sir!" he hissed through clenched teeth, and came in swinging, his arms windmilling furiously.

Kincaid made his move—such as it was. He simply dropped his guard and allowed one of Doyle's chaotic swings to connect with his jaw. He stumbled a bit, and Doyle shouted, "I'll show you, you bounder!"

The Englishman launched a wild roundhouse right that caught Kincaid on the side of the head, and the lieutenant went down!

A shout went up from the spectators, and the soldiers' mouths all fell open in utter disbelief. Lord Whitechapel began the count. Kincaid remained spread-eagled on his back through the entire count, at the conclusion of which Suzanne let out a jubilant shriek and ran to embrace her fiancé, who now had a wide but somewhat confused smile on his face. The soldiers came forward and crowded around their commanding officer, and Ben Cohen leaned close to him, saying, "Sir? Sir, can you hear me? Are you all right?"

Kincaid's eyes opened and he smiled broadly and winked at his first sergeant. "I'm fine, Ben, fit as a fiddle."

Cohen was so startled he nearly fell over. "Well, I'll

be goddamned!" he sputtered. "Why—?"

"Come on, Ben, you know why," Kincaid replied.

Cohen blinked in confusion, then smiled as the light dawned. "Diplomacy?" he said.

"You're catching on," Kincaid answered. He stood and dusted himself off as he looked toward where Doyle and Suzanne could be seen walking back toward camp, their arms around each other, surrounded by the rest of the Whitechapel entourage.

Later in the day they set out for the mountains once more. The land rose around them, the timber closing them in. The air was sweeter, cooler. Whitechapel was invigorated by it; Virginia continued to be bored by everything. Suzanne Ridgeley stuck close to her man, obviously proud of him. Doyle, for his part, seemed to have grown a couple of inches, and even smiled occasionally at Kincaid.

They camped that evening in a pleasant high meadow crossed by a winding silver rill. The grass was high and green, the wind off the mountain slopes cool, drifting the scent of pine and cedar to them.

There was still an hour of good light left when camp was pitched and Whitechapel took Farnsworth and Doyle off afoot on a hunt. Kincaid lay down in his tent, wondering what devilish impulse had ever encouraged him to take up army life.

"Yoo-hoo!"

Ben Cohen turned from his blanket roll and frowned. Lady Virginia Whitechapel was standing a little distance away, waving to him, and Ben walked that way suspiciously.

"Yes, ma'am?"

"We're nearly out of wood, Sergeant," she said, contriving to place a hand on Cohen's arm. "Could you, I wonder, provide some for us?"

Cohen looked around the deserted camp. The men had taken off into the woods to have a washup. He could, he supposed, go find them and order a woodcutting party out, but he decided to do it himself. He could use the exercise anyway.

"Yes, ma'am. I'll see to it."

"I happened to see a dead tree back up along that hill," Lady Whitechapel said, pointing breathlessly toward the timbered slopes.

What was going on here? Ben wondered. Finding Kincaid reluctant to play, was she going after Cohen now? He nodded his answer and said, "I'll get an ax and go on up."

"I could show you where it is."

"Not necessary," Ben said. He turned with the ax in his hand. Damn this woman! Was Ben going to have to be the next one to fight a duel? "I'll go alone."

He nodded again and strode past her, looking once across his shoulder at Her Ladyship, who stood, hands clasped, watching him.

With relief, Ben reached the verge of the forest and began looking around for dry wood. He found another small meadow and spotted a fallen cottonwood. Heading that way, he glanced to the empty, darkening skies, listening to the meadowlarks singing in the long grass. Beyond the meadow, the Medicine Bows thrust bulky shoulders against the skyline.

Ben peeled off his shirt and got to work on the cottonwood, the ax falling easily, methodically, biting deeply into the soft wood.

He started to whistle without realizing it, enjoying the exercise, the cool of the evening, the high-country silence.

116

"Oh, Sergeant!"

Ben turned in irritation toward Lady Whitechapel. The irritation quickly turned to horror. The lady had a furry bundle in her arms, stroking it, and as Ben recognized it for what it was, he started running that way, waving his arms frantically.

"Put it down! For God's sake, woman, put that bear cub down!"

She stood blinking at him, her hair drifting in the wind, petting the young grizzly cub. "Isn't it marvelous? Came right to me, Sergeant."

"Yes, and its mother will be coming right to us, too." Cohen reached for the cub and simultaneously heard the snuffling growl behind him.

He turned to see the massive grizzly rushing toward them, its loose coat moving across an immensely powerful body, its jaw hanging open to reveal yellowish fangs.

"Run!" Cohen knocked the cub from Lady Whitechapel's arms. The woman stood there, frozen by fear, and Ben shoved her hard. "Run!"

He spun back to face the grizzly, which was nearly on top of him, enraged and deadly. The cub, to Ben's frustration, had chosen to sit by his feet, unaware of anything.

The ax was in Cohen's hands. It wasn't much of a weapon against the charging bear, but he had no other. It was too late to run, too late to hide.

With a roar, the grizzly closed the gap between them, and Cohen, standing his ground, hefted the ax. As the grizzly lunged, Cohen struck.

The ax blade flashed downward with all of Cohen's strength behind it, and it bit deeply into the grizzly's skull. The animal died instantly, blood spurting onto Cohen's chest as the growl died in the animal's throat.

Its clawed forepaw rested inches from Cohen's boot, and he staggered back, looking with awe at the grizzly, the ax buried in its massive head.

The cub wriggled around, sniffing at its mother, bawling. Cohen sagged to the earth and sat there, unable to rise on those rubbery legs. That was as close as he had ever come, and he didn't want to come any closer. Cohen admitted to himself that he was ready to return to the orderly room and plant himself behind that desk for a good long time, to shuffle papers and bawl out the men, then close up in the evening and walk home to his good-natured, loving wife.

He heard footsteps rushing up behind him, and turned to see Whitechapel and Doyle coming on the run. Lady Whitechapel was gone.

"Jesus," Doyle breathed reverently.

"Ruined a damned fine trophy head," Whitechapel muttered, and stalked away, with Doyle following him.

Cohen stared after them, openmouthed, feeling numb. Then the numbness was replaced by anger as he looked down again at the cub, which was fruitlessly searching for a nipple in the belly fur of its dead mother. Cursing all the ignoramuses who seemed to find their way out to Wyoming Territory, he slowly drew his Scoff from its flapless holster and aimed it at the cub's head . . .

That evening was the first time Kincaid was to hear about the white buffalo robe. He had been invited to dinner, and he accepted. Doyle had chosen not to come, and Lady Whitechapel had been take with a case of the vapors following the incident with the grizzly. Cohen, Matt reflected, also had a touch of the vapors, of which the sergeant was endeavoring to cure himself with a pint of whisky.

118

Dinner was duck that Lord Whitechapel had taken that morning, glazed and sprinkled with almonds, along with pâté de foie gras and some sort of pudding Kincaid couldn't identify, which was thick with mushrooms.

"What about a white buffalo?" Lord Whitechapel said out of the blue, as they relaxed over brandy.

"Sir?"

"I say, have you ever heard of a white buffalo?"

"Heard of them, sir. Never have been privileged to see one, not even a robe. It's very big medicine to the Indians, you know."

"Magical properties?"

"Not exactly that, no, but certainly a valuable religious symbol to them."

"I understand their priests are buried in them," Whitechapel persisted.

"Not buried, sir, since the Plains Indians raise their dead on a platform. But, yes, I have heard that the truly great medicine men are sometimes laid to rest in a white buffalo robe, assuming there is one to be found. As I say, I have never seen such an article, and obviously they are so rare as to be uniquely valuable."

"I see." Lord Whitechapel changed the subject, leaving Kincaid to wonder exactly what the earl was getting at. He was still in the dark when Whitechapel rose from the table, his glass empty, and bade Kincaid goodnight.

"Been talking to Kincaid," Whitechapel told Virginia. She was propped up in bed, her long hair streaming across her shoulders in silken waves.

"Oh." Lady Whitechapel's voice was flat. The reluctant Kincaid was rapidly losing favor in her eyes.

"About the robe, you know. What a coup!" Whitechapel rubbed his hands together and made for the sideboard, where the brandy was set out nightly by Farnsworth. He poured a snifter half full and sipped at it.

"Have you talked to the Indian again?" Virginia asked.

"He's coming down tonight. Some sort of mystery about this business, but my God, will Bertram's face fall."

"And Lady Bertram. God, I'd love to see that bitch's expression."

"Please don't speak like that," Whitechapel said out of habit. His mind was on his triumph. "They'll likely have to add on a new wing to the Rutledge."

"The Whitechapel wing." Lady Virginia was as excited as her husband.

"Think of it! An American Indian chief—medicine man, whatever they call 'em—lying in state, wrapped in his sacred white buffalo robe. God!"

"How did this Twelve Sky fellow come to find this tomb?"

"Not a tomb, dear. Kincaid says they're buried aboveground, on platforms. Twelve Sky is the old medicine man's son-in-law."

"Then it's all aboveboard. It's all right?"

"Of course! Twelve Sky wants the rifle, which he has a use for. What on earth do any of them want with the corpse of a medicine man?"

"Ugh. Corpse. What a foul word."

"Mummy, then. That's actually what it is, you know. They have no use at all for it, but my God!" he exulted again. "Bertram will just howl with envy."

She was soft and near, her breasts pressed against his chest, her breathing soft, her hips slowly rising and falling, taking Malone along on a slow, undulating voyage across seas of pleasure.

120

"Nothing like an Irishwoman," Malone said, kissing Mary's ear, then lowering his lips to her breasts to toy with the erect nipples.

"Nothing like an Irishman," she murmured, yawning. "Wouldn't you like to go into service?"

"What's that?" he asked, lifting his eyes.

"Into service, you know, working for His Lordship."

"God, that's all I'd need." Malone pushed her hair back off her forehead and planted a kiss there. "I've enough trouble with the tyrants I'm used to. And I clean enough army pots without taking on the hundreds that Lord Whitechapel's chef uses every day."

"What's that?" Mary's voice was suddenly a taut whisper. She started to sit up, but Malone pressed her back against the grass, putting a finger to her lips.

"Where?" he whispered. Malone had seen nothing, but he had the instincts of a soldier. Rule number one was to stay down.

"Over there. By the tents. It was an Indian, I'm sure of it."

They lay side by side on their bellies. Malone's hand stretched out and closed around the butt of his Schofield pistol. He squinted into the shadows, seeing nothing. And then he did.

It was an Indian, to be sure, but he wasn't sneaking around. He walked upright, taking long, casual strides. Yet he paused as Malone watched, and looked around furtively. What in hell was he up to?

Malone frowned. The Indian walked to Lord Whitechapel's tent, and a faint voice seemed to welcome him. Then he was inside. Malone stared at the tent, puzzled.

"What was it?" Mary asked excitedly. She was slipping on her dress as she lay on the grass.

"Cheyenne. The one called Twelve Sky, I think."

"My God, he'll murder His Lordship."

"They seemed friendly enough."

"It's a trick, it must be."

"Maybe."

Malone watched awhile longer, then he slipped on his trousers and tugged his boots up, watching the tent all the while. No one was screaming bloody murder. There had been no sounds at all.

After he was fully dressed, he considered investigating, or at least reporting what he had seen to Kincaid. He had about made his mind up to go find Kincaid when a wedge of light fell across the ground before the duke's tent, and he saw Twelve Sky emerge, saw Whitechapel shake his hand, saw the Cheyenne turn and slip off into the darkness.

"Well, damn me, what do you figure that was all about?" Malone muttered to himself. "Come on," he said to Mary, "let's be getting back."

He tugged her to her feet, bent his head to kiss her one more time, and walked with her back to the tent city.

Yet his mind was not on the small, red-haired Irish girl, but on Indians creeping through the night. Something was up, but Malone couldn't hazard a guess as to what it was. He didn't like it, it didn't smell right, yet it was none of his business. At least he hoped not.

He said goodbye to Mary at the entrance to her tent, and walked off alone into the night to stand pondering it. Finally, able to make no sense of it, he forgot it. If Lord Whitechapel wanted to play with the Indians, it was his privilege, and if he ended up getting his aristocratic throat cut, it would be his own damn fault.

twelve ————————————

They traveled higher into the Medicine Bows, and though it was still summer below on the prairie, the mornings became cold, the days brisk and windy as they gained altitude. Lord Whitechapel wanted a big grizzly in the worst way, but he seemed impatient now, actually speaking of turning back. Matt couldn't figure it, and he didn't try. He stayed clear of the bunch of them as much as possible.

Lord Whitechapel and his people were gone from the base camp most of every day, still looking for a trophy-size grizzly. Kincaid had his men work a morning shift, cutting wood and doing the chores the camp manager asked to have done. The afternoons they had free. Cohen and Holzer used the time to do a little hunting themselves, while the rest of the men caught up on their sleep.

Kincaid found an icy little brook where the trout jumped in the morning sunlight, and he wondered if His Lordship had any angling gear with him. He lay back, taking off his shirt to soak up the sunshine.

She was there beside him so swiftly, so softly, that he hadn't even heard her coming.

He opened his eyes, seeing a lovely, haughty face framed loosely by honey-colored hair. Beyond her, the pine-clad mountains rose into the clear blue sky. The creek sparkled past, making musical sounds against the streambed rocks.

Matt closed his eyes again. He felt the soft hair brush against his cheek, felt her lower her body against his, and suddenly he didn't care. He was too damned tired for propriety, too much of a man to turn her away again.

He felt her fingers working on the buttons of his trousers, felt her lips cross his bare stomach. When she came to him again, her breasts were warm and soft against his chest as she straddled him, her eyes alight, her mouth slack and heavy.

Her lips met his, and Kincaid gave it up. He kissed her hard, feeling her shudder, feeling her lips part, her tongue searching for his, her hands clutching his shoulders.

The sun was warm. Her hair cascaded across his shoulders and chest as she bent to kiss his shoulder. He saw her smile, saw the concentration on her face as she scooted back, her hand searching for and finding him, closing around him with small, encouraging touches.

Then she lifted herself, positioned him, and settled again, nestling against Matt, who slipped easily into her warmth. Again she sighed. Matt saw her toss back her golden hair and sit erect, her breasts full and proud, her pale skin beautiful and smooth, her eyes distant, pleasure-filled.

She ran her hands across her breasts, over her own thighs, then dropped them between her legs to touch

Kincaid where he entered her, toying with herself, with him.

His hands dropped to meet hers, and their fingers intertwined, Kincaid gently stroking her, feeling her damp softness. The lady sat, head upright, her warm fingers encouraging him, pressing his hands against her.

She shuddered and spread herself even wider, the smooth, long muscles of her thighs going taut, and slowly she began to shudder, to slide against him, her pelvis meeting his, and she fell forward, her breasts flattened against his chest, her mouth hard against his, as she whispered frantic encouragement.

Kincaid's hands reached behind her, finding Her Ladyship's firm, smooth buttocks, finding the tender flesh where he entered her, and she trembled again.

She trembled and then seemed to come apart. Her body fell into a pitching, swaying motion, her hips working regularly, passionately, as her hot, cadenced breath sang in Kincaid's ear.

He lifted her higher, wrapping his arms around her, crushing her to him as his own head began to swirl and spin, as the thudding in his loins became an insistent, demanding drive.

She had begun to cry and laugh and moan all at once. She tore at him, grabbed for him, kissed him, begging for more until she threw back her head and screamed toward the exultant sky, coming to a slow, quivering rest as Kincaid finished his long, satisfying battle with a deliberate series of slow thrusts.

They lay silently, Kincaid stroking her hair. He realized he did not even know her, did not even *like* this woman who had needed him so badly, who had pursued him shamelessly.

He realized simultaneously that she was bored and

spoiled, that she was lonely and very young. Without the lovely gowns, the carefully coiffed hair, she seemed scarcely more than a girl, a girl married early to an older man who had as his single passion wandering the far lands.

He might not have felt deep affection for her, but at this moment, strangely, Kincaid felt pity. He held her close and let the sun drift overhead, the brook ramble by, the pines sway in the light breeze, and she slept, making small childish sounds as she dreamed.

When Matt awoke, it was already chilly. He dressed swiftly, stiffly. It somehow seemed to have been a dream, although he knew it had not been. They didn't make dreams so soft, so vivid, so satisfying.

There was excitement in the camp when Kincaid returned. Whitechapel, with his fully dressed, fully coiffed wife at his side, was standing before the hides of two massive grizzlies. They were stretched out to their full height on improvised wooden frames, their heads glaring down at the humans, who were as dwarves by comparison.

"There you are, Kincaid. Told you you were going to miss out one of these days. Look at this beggar! Fifteen feet if he's an inch. Stonebrook's gone for the tape; we'll soon see what sort of trophy we've got, though, by God, I believe this big fellow will top anything I've seen."

Kincaid muttered congratulatory words. He did not look at Virginia, nor she at him. From time to time she made a droll comment as she clung with a devoted wife's pride to her husband's arm.

Whitechapel was aware of none of the subtle byplay. He was a hunter, only a hunter. Maybe the man should have been born in a different age, or somewhere far from civilization, where he could have roamed the bush with a spear in his hand providing meat for the village, then dying in honored old age. Maybe, Kincaid thought with a sudden burst of insight, the old man too was bored, simply bored with life in the manor, with his teas and lordly obligations.

Whitechapel now stood flushed and tall and proud. He was in his element. Matt turned and walked back to where Easy Company was camped.

"How long's this go on?" Ben Cohen asked as Matt sat beside his sergeant, drinking a cup of coffee, while sundown streaked the skies with fire.

"You heard the captain. All summer, likely. What's wrong, Ben? I thought you were enjoying all this."

"Oh, I was, sir, and parts of it I still do like. It's sure a change of scenery, and the exercise has done me some good, I reckon. Maggie's been complaining that I was busting the seat out of my britches, going to lard from sitting behind a desk all day, every day. But it's enough of a good thing, I guess, and I got to admit I don't cotton to the airs these snooty folks put on. This is all a game to them, like lawn croquet or somethin'. They don't have to live here, they don't have to worry that any minute, just because he's wearing a blue uniform, a man might find an arrow between his shoulder blades and his hair gone. They can go out and shoot fifty, a hundred buffalo like it was nothin', never stopping to think that somebody's going to have to pay, either the Indians that could live for a whole season on the jerked meat and keep themselves warm with the hides, or the settlers and cattle herds that get raided by those same Indians so they won't starve to death or freeze, or the army that's going to have to fight those hungry Indians." He shook his head. "I don't know, sir, maybe I've gone soft in the head as well as in the butt. I never thought I'd hear myself say it, but

I'm missing old Number Nine, dreary as it is." *And Maggie too,* he thought, *familiar as she is. Familiar and fine.*

Kincaid clapped him on the shoulder. "Don't worry, Ben," he said, "you're not getting soft. You just know bullshit when you see it. Anyway, His Lordship seems restless. I don't know what's up, but I have an idea we won't be out as long as he originally planned."

Cohen looked up at Kincaid, brightening instantly. "Thank you, sir," he said. "I believe you've just made my day."

"Malone!" Reginald Dolittle had himself drawn up to his full height. He clicked his tongue dryly and came up to the soldier who was elbow-deep in dishwater, as he had been for weeks now. Dolittle held out a black iron kettle. "This is wretched. Now I know you're not a practiced scullery man, but we must have better work than this."

His fingernail flecked off a bit of dried food which was on the outside of the pot beneath the handle. Malone gritted his teeth.

"I'll try to do better."

"I should hope so. I realize it is difficult for you to apply yourself to this job. Your mind, I am sure, is drifting in other directions. Yes," Dolittle went on as he held up a hand, "I know all about you and the girl. You're both Irish; I've taken that into account and tried to ignore it."

"I'm American," Malone said, feeling his blood begin to heat up a little. Dolittle shrugged as if the distinction were nebulous.

"American, Irish—not proper serving material. Nevertheless, Malone, we must do better than this!" Dolittle placed the pot down beside Malone, wagged a finger at him, and turned away.

Pettigrew was just in time to keep Malone from picking up the pot and bouncing it off Dolittle's head. "Who in hell does he think he is! Some glorified butler who's likely never done a day's work in his life. By God, I'd like to—" Cooling slowly, Malone said, "Thanks, Pettigrew, I'd have cracked his skull for him for sure."

"All right," Pettigrew mumbled. He turned away and got to his drying.

"No brainstorms yet?"

Pettigrew came to life. "I've seen a herd of mustangs!"

"Yes?" Malone said cautiously.

"The mustangs. You remember, Malone. We talked about it before."

"Yes." Pettigrew obviously didn't recall Malone's lack of enthusiasm for the project the first time they had discussed it.

"In a high meadow not far from the camp! Why, if we could go out and rope some of them ... Only ten of them, Malone."

"Who is this 'we' you're talking about, Andy?"

"Why, you and me and the rest of the boys. Not Fremont, of course, but Holzer and Rafferty, Corson and you. Why, we could round up ten horses in an afternoon, I'll bet. Nobody's working in the afternoons anyway. What would it cost us? What would it cost the army? Nothing at all but a little time."

"Slow down a minute, Andy. God's sake, no one has said they're going to go off chasing wild horses with you, have they?"

"But you would?" Pettigrew's eyes were embarrassingly pleading.

"Does she really mean that much to you, Andy?"

129

Malone dried his hands on the towel Pettigrew was holding. He leaned against the table, folding his arms. "I mean, does this Sioux woman really mean all that much to you?"

"Dammit, Malone, I'm going to marry the woman!"

"Yeah." Slowly, Malone shook his head. He lifted his arms and let them slap against his thighs. "All right. I'll give it a try. I'll help you rope some of them mustangs."

"Malone!" There were actually tears in Pettigrew's eyes, and Malone grimaced painfully.

"Goddammit, Andy, let's get these dishes done," he snarled, turning away, cursing himself for a fool. But then, what good was a friend if he wasn't willing to help out? Not that they had a chance in hell of catching those mustangs, roping them, or herding them back to the outpost.

"There's plenty of grass," Pettigrew said excitedly. Malone didn't respond. "We can fix up some kind of a corral out of brush and boughs." Malone said nothing. "We'll rope them, gentle them out a little—you ever break horses, Malone?"

When there was no answer again, Pettigrew turned away with a sigh and got to work, his eyes distant and dreamy.

Holzer was easy to convince. He moved about animatedly. "To catch the wild horses, to throw them for Andy's feet, to marry the squaw! Good business," he said. "I like the business of the horses."

Rafferty didn't. Nor did Corson. They sat looking at Malone as if he were crazy. "Sure this isn't some wild scheme of your own?" Rafferty asked Malone, who had hatched a few wild ones in his time.

"It's for the kid, dammit," Malone said. "Christ, he wants to marry the Sioux lady, I figure we can try to help him. We've been with Andy for some time. I recollect him saving your butt once, Corson."

"Yeah," Corson acknowledged grudgingly, "he did. But dammit, Malone, I'm no wrangler, whatever in hell you call 'em."

"Mustanger."

"Yeah. All my horses have been broke for me by the army. What in hell do I know about roping wild horses, or taming 'em?"

"I'm just asking you to try," Malone said. "We'll do our best, and if it's not good enough, that's that. We'll have tried."

"To rope the strange horses!" Holzer shouted, waving his arms about.

"See, Wolfie's willing."

Corson looked morosely at Wolfgang Holzer. Of course Wolfie was ready; he was ready for anything, no matter how crazy. Corson looked back at Malone and slowly shook his head.

"I'm crazy, but I'm in. I guess it's like you say, we owe Andy a shot at it."

"Rafferty?"

"All right. I'm crazier than both of you. I *know* this is a fool's parade, but count me in. Find me a lasso, boys. I'm a wild horse hunter."

thirteen _____

They rode out of the base camp early the following afternoon. Pettigrew was as excited as a kid at Christmas. Holzer wasn't much less eager. Corson, Rafferty, and Malone all revealed various degrees of reluctance.

Lieutenant Kincaid had seen them, but he hadn't said anything. He seemed distracted by something. Cohen had asked what was up, but they had satisfied him by saying they wanted to see a little of the country. Fremont, who hadn't been invited and wouldn't have accepted if he had been, watched morosely as they headed into the big timber, their horses outfitted with Texas-rigged saddles borrowed from Lord Whitechapel's wranglers. Coils of new, stiff hemp rope were looped around the saddle-horns.

The forest was deep and dark. The horses' hooves whispered across the pine needle carpet beneath the trees. A cool whispering wind drifted down through the pines from the flanks of the Medicine Bows.

"How far are we going?" Rafferty asked.

Malone shrugged. "Ask the foreman. Odds are we won't find 'em at all. Those wild horse herds wander a bit, don't they?"

It was Rafferty's turn to shrug. "Maybe not, if they've got graze and water and nobody's been bothering them."

"We will throw them all at his feet," Holzer said confidently. He patted his rope and grinned at Malone.

"Wolfie, you're a jewel," Malone said under his breath.

"Prussian," Holzer objected, and Malone threw his hands into the air.

Beyond the forest lay the wide mountain meadows. They rode into the long grass, the horses' hoofs swishing pleasantly. They startled a masked badger, which turned and showed its teeth challengingly before scurrying away to its burrow. Larks sang all across the meadows, and crows called from the high sky where they circled lazily, black stains against the blueness.

"Look!" Pettigrew shouted, loudly enough to be heard back at the base camp, standing in his stirrups. Malone was jolted out of his pleasant memories of Mary McGuire, and he lifted his head to follow Pettigrew's pointing finger with his eyes.

"Sure enough. I'll be damned."

Two dozen wild horses stood watching their approach from a distance of nearly half a mile. Their heads were lifted alertly, and in another few seconds they took to their heels, starting left, then veering right, galloping across the open meadow, a flash of color and motion, wild and elusive.

"To capture them!" Holzer yelled, grabbing for his rope. Malone calmed him.

"They're too far off. We'd never catch them. Patience, Wolfie, patience."

They reined in to talk it over. Pettigrew's eyes were positively glittering. "Listen," he said, "this is wonderful. I scouted up that direction yesterday. They're running into a box canyon. They must think it's a safe place, but it's a trap. That canyon rises toward that peak, and I tell you they can't get out."

"They've sheared off," Corson observed. "They're heading west again."

"All right!" Pettigrew was nearly out of control. "All we've got to do is herd them toward the canyon. Half of us head west and the other half east. We'll work them between us and push them toward the canyon. Once we've got them inside, we've won!"

"Yeah," Malone said dubiously. If you didn't count the roping, the breaking, the herding, they would have it made. "All right." He looked over the men. "Corson? You and me to the west?"

"Whatever you say," Corson said with as little enthusiasm as Malone.

Together they retraced their tracks, angling slightly toward the sheer-sided peak that jutted skyward beyond the timber. Looking across his shoulder, Malone saw Pettigrew leading Holzer and a reluctant Rafferty to the east to try to head off the herd. Malone shook his head, letting Corson speak for him.

"It'll never work. Never."

The mustangs turned suddenly northward, bolting for freedom. Pettigrew's party rode like hell, trying to cut them off, but the majority of the mustangs broke free, running across the mile-long meadow away from the canyon.

Still, they managed to turn half a dozen of them. Wild-eyed, frantic, these mustangs turned in confusion and rushed back to the south, toward the canyon. Malone heard someone give a loud yahoo, and then, with a glance at Corson, Malone spurred his bay into a run.

The wild horses were near to Malone and Corson now, but seeing these two mounted men, they turned again, running back toward Pettigrew, who was closing the trap. One gray mustang broke past Malone and got into the forest, leaving five horses wheeling toward the canyon. Five would be half of what Pettigrew needed, Malone thought fleetingly, a good haul if they could actually trap them in the canyon, as Pettigrew believed.

Suddenly the canyon yawned before them, its high rocky bluffs parting to welcome the wild horses. Malone noticed the gray granite cliffs, the scattered pines, but his attention was on the wild horses.

One of them, he noticed, was in bad shape. Scrawny, with running sores on its flanks. All right, then—four horses for Pettigrew.

They met Pettigrew's party again. Holzer reined in sharply, his face exultant. He had his lasso out and was ready to go. The mustangs had vanished into the narrow canyon, following a right-hand bend.

"Corson, will you stay here to guard the mouth?" Pettigrew asked. "Maybe you can drag that deadfall over here to make a sort of barricade."

"Gladly," Corson said. "I don't want to try my hand at roping those wild-eyed bastards."

Malone tended to agree with him. But he found himself nevertheless with Pettigrew, Holzer, and Rafferty, riding into the canyon.

"That narrows out real quick," Pettigrew told them, indicating the canyon fork the mustangs had chosen. "We've got them now."

"Oh, yeah," Malone said softly. They had them all right, now what in hell were they going to do with them?

Pettigrew was forming a loop, and the others followed suit. They walked their horses up the rocky canyon bottom. Malone's horse was reluctant, not liking the smell of the wild horses, perhaps.

"There they are!" Andy Pettigrew shouted, and he was right. Four wild horses standing close together, ears pricked, eyes wary. Two of them were lanky and dust-colored, the third was a stubby roan, the fourth a spotted horse with an evil cast to its eyes.

"Choose one," Andy said. "I'll try the roan."

When they were finished choosing, Malone was left with the spotted horse, which looked as tough as nails and eager to prove it. They slowly fanned out, approaching the horses.

"On the feet, I think," Holzer said. No one answered him. They saw Holzer slip from his saddle and begin to approach on foot. The wild horses started to run, found they had nowhere to go, and milled about whinnying unhappily.

Malone let his bay have its head while he got his loop ready. It had been a long time since he had tried to rope anything, and he had no confidence in his ability.

Tugging his hat down, he took a deep breath and guided the bay toward the spotted horse. He watched the animal closely. It stood, legs spread, ears up, watching back.

The spotted horse let Malone get within fifteen feet before it set itself in motion, running hard toward the rising bluff. Malone's lasso snaked out, missed by five feet, and fell harmlessly to the ground.

He heard a yell behind him, and turned to see Holzer being dragged across the earth by a dust-colored horse. Somehow the German had roped the damned thing, but he wasn't doing much of a job at stopping it.

Malone forgot the spotted horse and turned the bay, pulling in his rope as he rode. Holzer's eyes were wide, his mouth open in a cry for help that they couldn't hear above the pounding of the hoofs.

Malone tossed his lasso, missed again, and cursed. He saw Holzer dragged against a huge rock outcropping and he thought the soldier would let go, but he clung to the line like a drowning man, continuing to yell. Malone was aware of other frantic activity behind him, but he paid no attention to it.

He threw his lasso again and this time, by God he scored. The loop settled around the mustang's neck, and Malone, with a quickness he thought he had long ago forgotten, threw a dally hitch around the pommel of the Texas-rigged saddle.

The dust-colored horse strangled out, its hind feet kicking out in frustration and anger. Malone's own horse, which was no cow pony, went to its hind legs, not understanding why it was tied to this other horse, this wild cousin.

Malone clung to the bay's neck and settled it slightly, though it continued to dance and shake its head. Malone dismounted, then worked his way down the line toward the wild horse, which reared and slashed out with deadly hoofs. Holzer was on his feet now, and Malone could see that his shirt was torn to rags, his hands bloodied. He was determined, though; you had to hand it to Holzer, he was always determined.

"To throw him down, Malone!" he shouted helpfully.

"Don't get any closer!" He looked round for help, and saw that Rafferty and Pettigrew were both busy with the other mustangs. "Get your horse, Wolfie!"

Holzer dropped his line and headed on the double for his bay. Mounting, he returned while Malone held the rearing wild horse with a single line. Holzer recovered his line and stretched it taut.

Now they had the wild horse between them, but their efforts did nothing to slow the mustang down. It went to its hind legs, snapped blindly at the tethering lines, and shook its head angrily. Malone began to snub his line down, drawing closer to the mustang. Holzer followed suit, watching to see how Malone was working the rope he had around his saddlehorn.

The mustang settled, quivering, and Malone took in still more slack. The wild horse shook its head, blew through the nostrils, and stamped its front feet against the hard ground.

"Now what in hell are we supposed to do with it?" Malone shouted.

"To ride it!"

"You ride it, you crazy ass!"

Holzer only grinned. He had had enough adventuring. Malone looked across his shoulder to see what Pettigrew was doing with the other horse, realizing that Andy's plan seemed a little incomplete.

Pettigrew had his loop around the roan's neck, but he sure didn't have it under control. It was bucking furiously across the floor of the canyon, raising clouds of dust.

Rafferty was having even worse luck. The spotted horse made a break for the canyon entrance, and Rafferty tossed his lasso on the run. From the look on his face, it surprised even him when his loop, arcing out, settled over the mustang's head.

Rafferty got the line over his saddlehorn and held on. As Malone watched, Rafferty jerked back the reins of his bay, setting the horse back nearly on its haunches. The spotted horse reached the end of the slack and kept on going. Rafferty's saddle popped free, and a horrified Rafferty was sailing through the air, sitting his saddle but not his horse.

He landed with a jarring thud, still clinging to his saddle. In another second he was free, rolling across the earth as the spotted pony ran on.

"Rafferty! Give us a hand!"

He looked up at Malone with glazed eyes. Rafferty was sitting, legs folded, arms dangling, staring at them, little bells ringing in his head.

Pettigrew had meanwhile lost his horse somehow, and was coiling his rope for another try. "Here!" Malone hollered, and Pettigrew rode toward them.

"Great! Terrific!" Pettigrew was shouting, and it was all Malone could do to keep from telling him how terrific he thought this was.

"What the hell do we do with him?" he asked angrily.

"Lead him along. There's a shallow fork up ahead. We can make a fence across the mouth of it."

"You hear?" Malone shouted at Holzer. Holzer nodded. "You understand?"

"To ride him!"

"Not yet." Malone closed his eyes tightly for a second. The wild horse had begun to cut up again, bucking, crow-hopping, twisting, as they held the lines taut. "Come on!"

Slowly they turned the mustang and dragged it to where Pettigrew sat waving them on. Malone saw the narrow feeder canyon now. It was deep but shallow. Pettigrew was already dragging brush and deadfall timber toward the mouth of the canyon, which was to be his makeshift corral.

The mustang was having none of it, but by main force they got the animal into the narrow canyon. They slipped their loops and got out of there, leaving an angry wild horse behind.

They helped Pettigrew close off the mouth of the canyon, building their barricade four feet high. The horse wouldn't attempt to jump out of there unless its tail was on fire. They could hear it whinnying pitifully, perhaps calling for its companions.

Rafferty was staggering toward them, carrying his saddle, the cinches cleanly snapped.

"Lost my horse," he said. His eyes were unfocused and dull. "Got to find my horse. Cohen'll have a fit."

"Sure, we'll find him. Climb up behind me," Malone said. Rafferty stared at Malone as if he had never seen him before, but he stepped up and clambered aboard Malone's horse.

"One down," Pettigrew said. "The rest will be in the big canyon. By God, I think this is going to work!"

It wasn't going to work, not on that day. The horses were long gone from the canyon. They found Corson holding Rafferty's horse at the mouth of the canyon.

"Gone," he said. "They came running down the canyon and they were by me. Over the barricade and out into the meadow."

Pettigrew's face fell, but he brightened again quickly. "We'll have to work around behind them again. It worked once, it'll work again. Malone, take the east side of the meadow—"

"Andy, I'd love to, but I got to get back and scrub some pots. I'll have people all over me if I don't show. Sorry."

"All right. Sure." Pettigrew turned toward Rafferty, who was still hearing bells.

"Who're you?" Rafferty asked.

"Holzer?" Andy began again. The German stood with his shirt torn to rags, his face and hands bloody, the knees torn out of his trousers.

"Andy, I cannot throw them down again."

Corson wouldn't even look at him. They saw Pettigrew's face fall, saw the frustration building. Malone spoke, wishing the moment afterward that he hadn't opened his big mouth again.

"Tomorrow, Andy, all right? None of us can take any more of this today. I got to get on back. Maybe tomorrow."

"Sure." He stepped into his stirrup and swung aboard, his optimism returning as they headed out into the meadow. "By God, we got one! Tomorrow we'll do better. We'll be better organized. I can't thank you boys enough! By God, I'll have those ten horses!"

He settled back into the saddle, daydreaming of Dawn Fox while Corson raked Malone with a savage look. Malone only shrugged and sighed. What was a man to do?

fourteen

The second day was, if anything, worse. Experience was apparently no guarantee of success in the mustanging business. Corson managed to get himself kicked in the leg, Malone nearly got trampled, but at the end of a long, long afternoon they actually had three horses in the canyon pen.

Pettigrew was in hog heaven. He had cut some hay out on the meadow for his ponies, and he stood gazing lovingly at them over the makeshift corral gate.

"Beauties, aren't they?" he said. Malone glanced at the ugly, stubby horses and shrugged. He was coiling his rope, hooking it over the saddlehorn. "We'll soon have 'em."

"Andy," Malone said quietly, "you know, Lord Whitechapel is liable to take a notion to move on any day now. The rate we're going, there's a good chance we won't have ten ponies before that happens."

"We'll have them," Andy said. "We'll have them because it's right. Because I belong with Dawn Fox."

A man couldn't argue with that kind of logic. Malone glanced at Corson and stepped into leather.

"Washing pots still?" Corson asked.

"I am."

"I heard Cohen wanted to rotate that duty. What's the matter with you, Malone? Why are you holding on to that job? Getting into His Lordship's liquor, are you?"

"Something like that." Getting into something much better, he thought, but he wasn't about to mention Mary McGuire.

"I think you're going soft." They rode out into the meadow again, Corson and Malone leading the pack.

"Yeah?"

"Yeah." Corson spat. "Look at you. Washing all them pots every night. Helping Pettigrew with this harebrained scheme. This ain't the Malone I always knew."

"I've always been generous and hardworking," Malone said with a straight face. "Loyal, courageous, and true."

"And full of shit," Corson said, wheeling his horse to the side before Malone's boot could reach him.

"What is going on?" Kincaid asked Ben Cohen as the five men rode into camp. Matt stood, hands on hips, watching them dismount and tend to their horses. He saw the saddles, which were definitely not army; they looked like cowboy rigs, presumably belonging to Whitechapel's people.

"Beats me, sir," Cohen answered.

"Did you see Holzer yesterday? He looked like he tangled with a grizzly."

Cohen winced. Any mention of a grizzly was apt to have that effect on him these days.

"I figured I didn't want to know, sir. It's their time. As long as they're not breaking any regulations, not disrupting the camp, I was letting them have their secret."

"You mean you asked and nobody would give you a straight answer."

Cohen grinned. "That's about it, sir."

Matt Kincaid grinned himself. "Seems there's always something going on that we don't know about, doesn't it?"

"When Malone's involved, sir," Cohen said soberly.

"He hasn't been in any trouble lately, has he?"

Cohen frowned thoughtfully. There was that Saturday night business—what that was, Cohen still didn't know. "Not here, far as I know. Been the perfect little gentleman. That Dolittle has been up complaining, but I know his sort. He's lucky Malone hasn't broken his face for him, and I'm not sure I could hold it against him if he did."

"Mm." Kincaid's thoughts had drifted away from Malone and Pettigrew, from Dolittle and Cohen. He had seen a young woman with honey-blond hair walking into the forest, seen her pause and look expectantly toward the Easy Company camp.

"I believe I'll take a stroll," Kincaid said. "Stretch the legs a little."

"Yes, sir," Cohen said, remembering not to smile. He watched Matt Kincaid head off toward the pines. Then, turning away, he began to whistle. Malone and Pettigrew had their secrets. Matt Kincaid wasn't so good at keeping his.

She was warm and soft against him. The shadows of the pines lay across her body. She stretched out a hand and touched Kincaid's lips.

"This won't last long enough. It will be ended far too soon," Virginia said. "My husband wants to head back toward the outpost within three days."

144

"He does!" This was news to Kincaid. Virginia kissed his bare chest and drew him down again. "Why?"

"He's made arrangements to meet someone. The Indian."

"Twelve Sky?"

"Yes." She kissed him, stifling all conversation for a moment. Her hands roamed Matt's naked thighs interestingly.

"Whatever for?"

"I can't say. It's a secret."

"Everyone's got secrets in this outfit."

"Yes," she said with a smile. She lay back and spread her arms out. "But ours is the sweetest." Matt, going down to her, was in perfect agreement.

Malone got the word from Mary McGuire, although under less agreeable circumstances. He had the brass brush out and was working intently at the iron pots when Mary, delivering a stack of dirty plates, paused to stand over him.

"We're heading back soon, Mr. Malone."

"Back?"

"Back to your fort. His Lordship is all heated up about something. I heard him and Mr. Doyle talking about it."

"I thought he was going to stay up here for a long while, another month at least."

"And so he was, but something's come up." Mary brushed her hair back from her eyes.

"Damn!"

"You'll miss me that much?"

"Huh? Of course I will. You know that, Mary. But I was thinking of Pettigrew."

"What do you mean?"

Malone told her the story of Dawn Fox and the ten ponies, told her what they had been doing all day, and

145

Mary, arms folded beneath her breasts, nodded sympathetically.

"The poor man. I wondered why he paid no attention to any of the maids. I thought maybe he was one of them funny boys. He's in love, is he? And a desperate love."

"That's what it is. Whitechapel didn't say how long we have, did he?"

"Three days, I believe. Will that give you enough time?"

"Not the way we're going," Malone said ruefully.

"If I could do something to help, I would," Mary said sincerely.

"There's not much, I'm afraid."

"Can't the men chip in and give him money to buy horses?"

"They might, if there was a dime among us. It's been a long while since payday. No, it's got to be the mustangs."

"Then I wish you luck, Mr. Malone." She came to him and kissed him lightly. "If anyone can do it, it's you who will help him, I know that."

Malone wished he were so confident. He was stiff and weary, as were the others. The wild horses were wary now, knowing these men were up to no good. The whole thing seemed less probable the longer he thought about it.

"Private Malone." The voice was Dolittle's, and Malone winced. That was all he needed. Dolittle pranced up to him and, looking over his shoulder, shook his head with great sadness. "This won't do, Malone. We must apply ourselves to our work."

"Yes, Mr. Dolittle," Malone said through clenched teeth.

"After all, this is not a country vacation for you, is

it?" Dolittle paused. "And someone has been in the liquor. Did you know that?"

"How would I know it? I don't even know where the damn stuff is kept."

"No? I've been making inquiries about you, Private Malone. You're known for this sort of antics, you realize." Dolittle was nearly in Malone's face.

"People have gotten themselves punched for pushing me too hard, Dolittle," Malone warned him.

The Englishman fell back, astonished. "So! This is the way you speak to me! Bald threats. By God, I'll report you. Wait and see if I don't." With that he scurried away, leaving Malone and Mary McGuire alone.

"I wish you *had* punched him," she said. "The man's an ass."

"It doesn't do any good," Malone said with wisdom born of bitter experience. "Still, sometimes..."

"He's left a wife at home. I think that's his trouble," Mary commented.

"Ah, a woman," Malone said lightly. "I knew it. If you look deep enough, there's always a woman at the root of a man's troubles."

"Yes?" Mary walked to him and leaned against him. "And who do you think causes a poor woman's troubles?"

"You're right," Malone laughed. "We're not exactly suited for each other, are we?"

"In ways," she said, "in certain ways. Do those pots now, you brute of a man, and I'll show you what I mean before this night is over."

"Ah, she knows how to inspire a man," Malone said, and he got to it again.

Pettigrew had come in, looking unhappy. He placed the dishes and silver on the table. Someone had let the air out of him.

"What's the matter?"

"Haven't you heard? We're leaving within three days. God, Malone, you were right. I haven't a chance."

"Did I say that? Well, I was wrong. You showed me I was wrong," Malone said with a grin. "We've got three of 'em, and damn me, we'll have the rest. We'll break those bastards and lead 'em back tame as kittens."

"But you—"

"Don't listen to what I said, listen to what I'm saying! I've seen the light, Andy. We can't fail. Man, it's meant to be, like you were saying all along." Malone took Pettigrew by the shoulders and shook him. Gradually, Andy brightened.

"Think so?"

"I *know* so," Malone said, knowing nothing of the kind. Pettigrew smiled and got to work. The conversation had left Pettigrew somewhat bolstered, and Malone feeling like a liar and a cheat.

"You poor dumb bastard," Malone said under his breath, "counting on Holzer and Rafferty, Corson and me for help." That's just what he was doing, of course, counting on his friends. Dammit, how could they let him down!

"We won't," Malone promised himself. "We won't." And all the time he was wondering just *how* they wouldn't.

They rode out again the next day, a little earlier this time, cheating on their camp duties, slipping out before Cohen could corner them.

It took them almost three hours to find the mustang herd. They were nervous and shy of human scent now. They refused to run for the canyon, but Corson, with some neat work that surprised everyone, managed to rope the spotted horse from his own horse's back at a dead run.

148

With the help of the others, he fought it to a standstill. They drove a long picket pin into the earth and left the mustang tied there.

"Can't leave him long, he'll chew through the rope," Corson reminded them. He looked back proudly at the horse, which hadn't yet figured that out and now stood eyeing them hatefully.

A mile farther on, they came on the main herd. Carefully they pushed them back toward the canyon, not wanting them to break into an all-out run. With luck and some skill they managed to get three more into the canyon. Corson and Holzer had returned for the spotted horse, and it was led with surprising ease into the canyon corral while the others went after those that had not been roped yet.

It was getting on toward evening, and Malone, thinking of Dolittle, winced. But there were three more horses in that corral, six altogether. Pettigrew reminded them of that every few minutes.

"Six, by damn! I've got me six horses."

Six horses, and they had two more afternoons to rope and pen four more.

"How's he know Black Hatchet, or whatever his name is, hasn't already moved in while Pettigrew's been gone?" Rafferty asked.

"He don't. That would be a bitch, wouldn't it? After all this."

"It's possible, Malone. Very possible."

"Don't I know it. Whatever you do, don't bring that thought up when Andy's anywhere around. It'd sink him, Rafferty."

Dolittle was fit to be tied. He went around waving his arms, shouting that Americans were unreliable, that Irish were lazy, that an Irish-American *soldier* was the lowest,

149

laziest most unreliable creature walking God's earth.

Malone, surprising himself, took it all calmly, but he was starting to have some very evil fantasies involving Dolittle.

He looked at the pots, feeling weary. His back and shoulders hurt from the day's work. His head ached dully. He hadn't eaten since breakfast. But then he looked up, saw that red-haired, smiling girl and he managed to forget about Dolittle, about Andy and his damned horses. The pots were only a minor inconvenience standing between Malone and a fine evening. He got to it with enthusiasm.

Morning was cool, the grass frosted. They crawled out of bed stiff and hungry. Malone sat red-eyed and numb on a fallen log, holding his coffee cup in shaking hands.

"Malone?" Cohen said. "Are you all right?"

"Fine."

"What time did they let you off work last night? You look like hell."

"I don't know. Late."

Surprisingly, Cohen rested a hand briefly on Malone's shoulder. Malone didn't seem to notice it. He looked exhausted, but you had to hand it to him—he still managed to smile, even after a hard night's work.

They drifted out even earlier that day, the next to the last. Pettigrew was showing the strain. Malone was jolted awake as his horse misstepped. He had been sleeping in the saddle.

He shook his head and looked around him. Pettigrew had held up and the others sat watching him. He turned and slowly nodded.

Malone, wiping the sleep away from his bleary eyes, saw them too—eight horses standing in the high meadow grass, their heads lifted. They were off again.

fifteen

Somehow they did it. It was grueling, impossible, fantastic, but they did it. By the time sunset was streaking the skies above the canyon, Pettigrew was able to look into this makeshift corral and count his ten horses.

"Ten!" He was exultant. He broke into an impromptu dance. He kept slapping them on the shoulders, telling them they were the greatest friends a man ever had. "I've got them. I've got them!"

"He's got 'em," Corson said sourly. Then he smiled despite himself. "Now all we got to do, old buckaroo, is break the beasts. All of 'em. In one day. What do you think of that?"

"I think," said Malone, "Dolittle is going to chew my ass out."

It was an accurate prophecy. The Englishman was incensed. Hadn't he just warned Malone? God, would he

151

be glad when they left Wyoming, when he could find some reliable help!

Malone, chin on his hand as he leaned on the table in the scullery tent, just yawned. He washed the pots and pans lethargically. Hell, there was nothing to this. Just wait until morning—that was some real work.

Malone's prophecy was accurate once more.

Breaking all rules this time, they rode out at dawn. The horses were there, looking mournful in the morning light. Mournful and dangerous.

"Well, who's the cowboy?" Malone asked.

"To ride the wild horses!" Holzer said.

"That mean you're volunteering?"

"I am the volunteer horseback."

"I'm the volunteer horse's ass," Rafferty said. "I'll try one too. God damn if I'll see all this work go down the drain now."

They unsaddled and left their own horses to graze. Cautiously they crept into the corral, Malone and Corson with ropes in hand.

The wild horses eyed them suspiciously and tried to run. There was nowhere to go in the close confines of the feeder canyon, and before long Malone and Corson had their loops around the spotted horse's neck. It stood shuddering as Pettigrew approached it, tossed his blanket up over the horse's eyes, and gestured frantically to Rafferty.

Rafferty, his mouth twisted into an unhappy grimace, approached the horse, threw his own saddle blanket over the spotted mustang's back, and smoothed it, talking softly to the animal. The saddle was next.

The cinches were tightened and Rafferty took the big step. Into leather.

"Let him loose!"

Pettigrew whipped the saddle blanket away and the

spotted horse was off. Crowhopping, twisting, bucking, going to its hind legs, leaping high to land stiff-legged, trying to jolt this foul-smelling two-legged creature from its back. But Rafferty stuck.

For all of thirty seconds. Then he did an imitation of a fizzling pinwheel, flying through the air to land hard against the ground as the spotted horse shook its head triumphantly.

Rafferty started to rise and Malone held him down. "Take it easy, boy."

"Damned if I will! This just got personal." He turned and pointed a finger at the spotted mustang. "It's you and me, you son of a bitch. You can't do this to me!"

He could—and did, three more times. Rafferty staggered to his feet each time. He was hatless, dust-coated, his face perspiration-streaked. But he climbed aboard again.

"Let him go," he said, and they did, reluctantly.

The spotted horse leaped and spun, but it was wearing down, giving up, and they cheered spontaneously as they saw that Rafferty was going to stick. By God, he was going to beat that horse!

He stepped trembling from the horse's back, gazing at it in admiration and awe. He walked around the horse and took its muzzle, stroking it. The horse tried once to nip him, but Rafferty slapped its muzzle hard. Then he stroked it again, grinning hugely at the others.

"Great," Malone muttered. "Now do the other nine."

And they did. Each man took a turn at it. They worked through the day, a day that was a constant swirl of dust, a jolting that clicked teeth together, rattled the spine, shook a man's guts loose. It was a sudden, brief flight through the air, a jarring impact, a narrow escape from slashing hoofs. But they kept at it. This was the last day, as Rafferty had said, it was finish the job or see all that

153

had gone before go down the drain.

No one mentioned that it might already be too late. Pettigrew had been gone for a long while. Black Hatchet was back there making love to his woman.

If Dolittle yelled at Malone that night, Malone was too tired to hear it. Truth to tell, he was even too tired for Mary McGuire, but he bore up. He staggered to his bed later, seeing the men spread out across the ground like the dead after a battle. Except for Andy Pettigrew.

He was sitting up, hands around his knees, looking at the stars.

"You boys are the best, Malone," Andy said. "The very best. A man doesn't forget this. I won't, not the rest of my life. You are the best." Pettigrew's voice caught, but Malone never heard it. He was sound asleep, dead to the world.

"Sir?"

Matt Kincaid, who had been having morning coffee with Ben Cohen, turned to see Private Pettigrew, his face scrubbed and shaved, but badly scratched, bruised on the cheekbone.

"Yes, Pettigrew?"

"I need to talk to you about something."

"Go ahead." Matt glanced at Cohen.

"It's about some horses." Pettigrew plunged into the story, growing more excited as he went along. When he got to the end of it he was breathless, flushed. "So the thing is, sir, I suppose I should ask if it's all right to take them along back to the outpost. So I am. You see?"

"Private Pettigrew," Matt said soberly, "look behind you and tell me what you see."

Andy did so. Lord Whitechapel's men were striking the tents. The wagons were being loaded. "Camp's breaking up, sir."

"That's right." Kincaid smiled. "You'd best get your confederates rounded up and go get those horses before you're left behind!"

"Yes, sir! Thank you, sir. They won't be any trouble, Lieutenant Kincaid." Pettigrew was backing away, saluting. Suddenly he turned and broke into a run, and they could hear him yelling, "Malone! Holzer!"

"Funny, ain't it, sir?" Cohen said, tossing the dregs of his coffee into the fire to hiss and steam.

"Pettigrew and his Indian woman?"

"No, sir, not that. Lord Whitechapel. He was all set to hunt through the summer and fall up here. Got provisions for another two months, easy. Yet suddenly he ups and decides the hunt's over."

"I have no complaints whatsoever," Matt answered.

Cohen grinned. "Nor have I, sir. I'll be honest, I've had more than enough. I'm more of a settled man than I thought. Bless the captain for sending me out. He showed me something, namely that I belong behind my desk, running this show from the orderly room. I'm too old or too damned set in my ways for this crap." Cohen winked, kicked dirt onto the fire, and walked off to find Fremont, who would have to be in charge of folding up the army tents, since Kincaid had let the others go after Pettigrew's wild horses.

Matt stood a minute longer, staring down through the pines at the camp, wondering again just why they were breaking camp now. It had something to do with that scoundrel Twelve Sky, Matt was fairly sure, but just what, he did not know. Nor would he, until it was too late to stop it.

Fremont was folding the lieutenant's tent and that of Sergeant Cohen, complaining all the while. He was the only one who did any work in this outfit. Only him. The rest of them were off playing some sort of game; no one

155

had even told Fremont what was up. They had pushed him out of the inner circle. All because he had told that damned Indian-lover, Pettigrew, what he thought of him.

Well, it wasn't over. Fremont was damned if it was over yet. "You've still got a surprise or two coming to you, Private Pettigrew," he said to himself.

Lord Whitechapel's experienced and efficient crew had the aristocrat's camp packed up with surprising quickness, and Whitechapel, bathed and attired splendidly as always, was standing, watching the last gear stowed away, the last lines tied, when Kincaid came up to him.

"All ready, Lieutenant?" His Lordship asked.

"Shortly, sir."

"I don't see your soldiers."

"No, sir. I've sent them on an errand."

"Yes." It didn't seem an odd explanation to Whitechapel. His mind was obviously somewhere else. He turned suddenly toward Kincaid. "I've been meaning to talk to you about this business between you and my wife."

Kincaid's heart fell two feet. The blood began to pound in his temples. His face felt hot. Lord Whitechapel's expression was wooden. He stood tapping a riding crop against his high boots.

"Sir?"

"No need for games, Kincaid. God, man, don't you think it's obvious! I'm a man who knows his wife. She moves differently now. She seems more feminine, softer, more languid. Her eyes are misted. She's positively feline, Kincaid. I know damned well who's responsible— and I thank you for it."

"Sir?" Kincaid goggled at the Englishman. His voice was a squeak rising from a dry, constricted throat.

"I appreciate it, man. You know, a man my age . . . well, let's say I'm not as young as I used to be, not so . . . able, if you know what I mean. Virginia's a young woman. Bored to death, I daresay, with this traipsing around the country. Well, a woman needs a man's attention, don't you think?"

"I suppose so, sir."

"I know damned well she does!" Whitechapel roared. "You're a gentleman, Kincaid. I realized that when I saw the capital way you handled that tricky business with Doyle. But good Lord, man, I thought you'd never break down and give her what she wanted! She was hell to live with, all pins and needles and broken glass. Now, well, she's content again, and I thank you for it."

With that, His Lordship thrust out his hand and Kincaid, numb and astonished, took it. Then Lord Whitechapel turned, shouting something at Farnsworth before calling for his horse, striding off toward the camp, leaving Kincaid to stand and stare blankly at the mountains.

From the east, Kincaid heard the sound of many horses walking through the pine forest and he turned to see his blue-clad cowboys coming in. The mustangs, all restless and recalcitrant, were strung together on a long leader that Pettigrew held on one end, Malone on the other. Corson, Holzer, and Rafferty, all looking well pleased with themselves, rode behind the wild horses, urging them along with whistles and yells.

Matt walked that way, watching as Pettigrew drew up. "This is them, sir," he said proudly, and Matt nodded.

"Fine-looking stock."

"Think so, sir? Good enough?" he asked anxiously.

"By God, Pettigrew, Big Nose will welcome you into the family with open arms! They're fine animals, and you've a right to be proud."

Pettigrew gave Kincaid a look of gratitude that embarrassed the officer. Malone was grinning, and Matt had to shoot him a stiff glance.

"His Lordship's ready," Ben Cohen said, slipping up beside Kincaid. He held the reins to Kincaid's saddled horse.

Matt look around and said, "It looks as if we are too, Sergeant. Let's turn this parade back toward Number Nine."

sixteen _____

The long plains stretched out before them, the grass dry and brown, shifting in the wind. Lord Whitechapel's wagons rolled on while the earl himself rode to the right flank astride that magnificent black gelding.

Virginia was riding horseback this morning, sidesaddle on a sorrel horse with a white tail. When Kincaid drew near enough, she fixed wistful eyes on him. The picnic was over, however. It was done, and Kincaid was both relieved and regretful.

Pettigrew trailed the long column, looking weary and euphoric. Malone helped him with the string of mustangs, which were nearly broken to the trail now, no longer fighting the lead rope. Holzer, Rafferty, and Corson were in high spirits. They too had had enough of this expedition and were glad to be heading home, as rough and uncomfortable as "home" was.

Fremont rode alone, his face sullen and dark, brooding.

Ben Cohen took it all in. The wind shifted the prairie grass and cooled the members of the expedition as the warm sun beamed down. The land he saw around him was raw and wild and quite beautiful. And he had seen enough of it, he decided.

They came up on Lacrosse Coulee at sunset, and made a hasty camp there. A hasty camp, for His Lordship, meant only six tents, including of course the fifty-footer, which was indispensable, having his bed and bathtub, wine racks and dining table in it.

Kincaid found Pettigrew near the fire. The young enlisted man came to his feet as Matt approached.

"I need a volunteer to ride ahead and inform Captain Conway that we'll be arriving late tomorrow evening or early the next morning."

"Yes, sir. I'd be happy to. But my horses—"

"You'd better take them with you, Pettigrew," Kincaid managed to say casually. "Find someone to go along with you and head for Number Nine. If you need to stop off somewhere and deliver those horses, that's all right. Can't have them at the outpost, you know."

Kincaid's voice was formal, bordering on sternness, but Pettigrew wasn't taken in. Impulsively he took Kincaid's hand. "Thank you, sir. Thank you. Is it all right if I take Malone?"

"If he'll go."

Malone, who was washing pots at that moment, was glad to go. He threw down his apron, kissed Mary McGuire, and stalked out of the tent with Dolittle on his heels, screaming frantically.

"It'll be a long ride, Malone," Pettigrew warned him. "I mean to go straight through. I can't stand this waiting and not knowing any longer. If you want, I'll ask Holzer to go, I know he would."

"Yes, and you should know I will too," Malone growled. "Dammit, I've a lot of time and effort invested in this romance. I want to see the end of it my own self." He winked at Pettigrew and slapped him on the shoulder. "Let's get ourselves into that Tipi Town and watch the expression on the old man's face when you show him these mustangs."

They rode out within the hour, when the first stars were blinking on in a hazy sky still stained orange to the west above the distant Rockies—Malone and Pettigrew and the ten horses that were the marriage price demanded by the old and honored Sioux warrior.

Pettigrew rode at a furious pace until Malone, dropping his end of the line, circled toward Andy. "Slow up, Pettigrew!" Malone told him. "God, man, you'll want to have these beasts alive when you get there."

Andy slowed slightly, but before they had gone another mile he had the string of horses moving at a gallop again, and Malone could only settle into the saddle, wondering at the ways of true love.

By midnight the moon was rising silver above the prairie, and the horses were exhausted. Malone was reeling in the saddle. He couldn't believe it when Pettigrew finally admitted he had had enough. They unsaddled and moved from their horses, rolling out their blankets on the moonlit grass.

"An hour's rest," Andy said. Malone's answer, fortunately, was inaudible. "An hour, and then we'll head on in. A little slower. By dawn we should be to Number Nine. By dawn I'll have spoken to Big Nose."

"Assuming he's crazy enough to get up with the sun," Malone muttered.

161

"By dawn it'll be settled, and the hell with Black Hatchet!" Andy leaped into the air, astonishing Malone. He flung his clenched fist overhead and performed a wild little hop-stepping dance. Malone watched him through bleary eyes, shaking his head. This man was not going to sleep on this night. He was sky-high. With Malone it was a different story. He had had enough, and he rolled up in his blanket, not wanting to waste a second of his allotted hour.

Andy Pettigrew paced the ground excitedly for long minutes. He peered northward toward Number Nine, but it was too distant to see. Then, as if performing some ritual, he walked to where his mustangs were tethered and counted them one by one, laying a hand on the flank of each horse.

Later he sat near his blanket, listening to Malone snore, watching the silver moon coast past against an inky sky, hearing the horses quietly cropping grass, the crickets singing in the distance.

Dawn Fox. He thought only of her, and remarkably he was able to summon to his mind a perfect image of her face. He was able to recall the close warmth of her body, her gentle ways, and he gave in to the soft reveries. He was asleep ·in her arms, her soft breathing in his ears . . .

Pettigrew sat up with a start. He had somehow fallen asleep. He looked around quickly. No, he was still dreaming, because the horses were gone, and he knew they were there, had to be there!

Andy staggered to his feet. Wiping the sleep away, he rushed to where the horses had been tethered. They must have broken the tether and wandered.

Gone!

"Malone!" Pettigrew turned in a slow circle, dazed and confused. "Malone!" he yelled again, only to find

162

that Malone was already beside him, rifle in hands.

"What is it?"

"The horses." Andy's hand rose and fell. He looked out across the dark plains, his head throbbing. "They must've broken the tether. Funny, I had it tied . . ."

"Wasn't that, Andy." Malone was crouched down. By the light of the dwindling moon he showed Pettigrew the moccasin tracks. "Indians got 'em. Slipped right up on us and took 'em from under our noses."

"No." Andy couldn't admit it. "We've got to find them. They can't have gotten far."

He was starting for his horse. Malone had to grab his arm. "Andy, we can't do a thing about it. Maybe when the sun comes up we can track them, but not now." Malone was silent and thoughtful. "Funny, they didn't take the army mounts."

"Afraid the U.S. brand would get them in trouble," Andy suggested.

"Maybe. That means they weren't hostiles."

"What?"

"A hostile wouldn't give a good damn if he was riding an army-branded horse, would he? Also, it's a good bet they would have scalped us. It would have been as easy as pie."

"Friendlies?"

"Looks like. Agency Indians, maybe . . ."

"Black Hatchet!" Pettigrew shouted. He clenched his fists and shouted it. "It was Black Hatchet, I know it was!"

"Maybe," Malone said. "Maybe him, maybe friends of his. It could be, Andy, and if it was, we've a good idea where to look for those missing ponies."

"Sure. You're right, Malone. Hostiles could be anywhere out there. If it was friendly Indians, they could only be at the agency or in Tipi Town." Pettigrew was starting toward his saddle, leaving Malone to sigh, look down at the faint tracks, and follow him.

They rode out at a slow walk, following the tracks left by the string of horses. The moonlight was thinning out as the moon sunk behind the mountains. Fortunately, dawn came on the heels of the darkness, and they were able to track faster within an hour.

They could see Outpost Number Nine off in the distance now, like a memory come to life. They followed the tracks all the way to Grand Coulee—and promptly lost them.

Along the sandy bottom of the coulee there were no definite tracks. There were many indefinite ones, some left probably by army patrols, others by gathering Indians. They rode north along the coulee bottom as the sun rose higher, warming their shoulders. Nothing.

They had gotten into heavy brush, and it was obvious no horses had passed that way recently. The brush would have been broken down. To the south they had no better luck.

"He led them out somewhere along here," Andy said, wiping his forehead with his sleeve. "If we track along the rim, we're bound to come across the tracks."

They did search along the rim, but they found nothing. It was getting on toward noon, and Andy's temper was getting as hot as the noonday sun.

"The bastard," Pettigrew said, looking toward Tipi Town. "I don't need to track the horses. I know who took them, and by God, he'll tell me."

"Easy, Andy," Malone said. He was taking a long drink from his canteen. "Fact is, you don't know anything of the sort. We *guess* Black Hatchet was involved. We don't know it."

"I'll make him admit it!"

"You will?" Malone nodded. "You're going to find

him and start beating up on a friendly Indian, you wearing army blue? Not likely, Andy. You'd raise a shitstorm, and you know it."

"He did it!"

"Likely, but we've no proof. You got to face it, Andy, you can't go after Black Hatchet without some proof. We'll ride over there and have a look around. Then we've got to report to the captain. After that—well, I don't know what to do after that."

Pettigrew had ceased to listen. He sat his horse, staring across the prairie, feeling empty and cheated and angry. Malone slapped him on the shoulder. "Come on, boy, let's do what can be done."

Malone knew this would come to nothing. What kind of damned fool would take those horses from a soldier and then lead them into Tipi Town, right next to Number Nine? No, the horses were hidden away nicely somewhere. And Andy Pettigrew had just been beaten.

Nevertheless, he followed Andy into Tipi Town, where they rode past suspicious and solemn dark eyes to Black Hatchet's tipi.

"You took my horses!"

"No. Soldier don't have horses."

"Damn you, Black Hatchet, you took my horses!"

Malone thought Pettigrew was going to go after him, but he didn't. Perhaps he knew by now that it was useless. Black Hatchet was expressionless, but his eyes seemed to hold a glint of triumph. Maybe it was Malone's imagination.

After a minute they rode back out, and from the corner of his eye, Malone saw the pretty young Sioux woman staring after Andy Pettigrew.

It was over.

Malone stumped into the orderly room to find Gus

165

Olsen looking harried and exhausted. Papers were all over his desk, and Olsen looked ready to pull his hair out.

"Malone!" Olsen looked beyond his shoulder.

"Not yet, Sergeant," Malone said, "but he's coming in. Kincaid says tonight or tomorrow morning."

"Thank God," Olsen breathed, sagging into Cohen's chair. "I used to envy Ben, thought he had it made over here. Now I wonder how the man ever kept his sanity."

"I think Cohen is anxious to get back here, Gus. Maybe everybody learned something."

"Including you?" Gus asked, only half jokingly. "Seems you never learn anything, Malone."

"Hell, I already know it all. Anybody'll tell you that." With a grin, Malone went to the captain's door and rapped on it.

Conway received the news of the return of His Lordship's party warmly. The man was going home, and early too. By the day after tomorrow he would be out of this area, another responsibility off Conway's shoulders. No more worries about the civilian and his party.

There was no way the captain could have known that his troubles with Lord Whitechapel were just beginning.

Whitechapel had made camp early in the afternoon, surprising Kincaid. His Lordship, his wife, Farnsworth, and Doyle had ridden out an hour after camp was made, Farnsworth riding on an open wagon beside a uniformed driver.

"What do you suppose that's about?" Cohen asked.

Matt shook his head. There was no telling, and if it didn't concern him, he didn't want to try to guess. But it was to concern him very soon.

Lord Whitechapel looked around him as he rode, liking the sweep of prairie, the distant mountains. The land

166

was so different from his native England. In a way, this was more his sort of country. He had never really felt at home in the civilized English countryside. Here a man was free, depending on his shooting eye and his own resources. He turned his head to study Virginia, who rode her little sorrel pony, her eyes dull, reflecting her boredom. This was no life for a woman. At times he wondered why he had married her, except to try to produce an heir. That had failed. Alvin Whitechapel would never have a son and heir.

"There he is, sir!" Farnsworth lifted an arm to the distant group of men, and Whitechapel urged his horse into a trot, riding more quickly toward the waiting Twelve Sky.

The man had three warriors with him, and an outsized bundle covered with blankets. Whitechapel stepped from his black horse and walked toward the bundle. He reached for the blankets, but Twelve Sky stopped him.

"You have guns?"

"Certainly."

"Let me see."

Whitechapel lifted a beckoning finger, and Farnsworth stepped from the wagon, went to the tailgate, and returned with two gun cases. These were placed on the ground, and Twelve Sky crouched to open the latches and examine the magnificent custom-made weapons. He stood with the Rigby .480 in his hands, put it to his shoulder, and pointed it directly at Whitechapel, who was too calm a customer to flinch.

"Satisfied?" the earl asked.

"Bullets."

"After we have looked," Whitechapel said. He wondered if Twelve Sky had any idea that these rifles would be worthless to him soon. The ammunition was unavailable in the United States, and after he had burned up the rounds the weapons would be nothing but pretty and very expensive toys.

Whitechapel moved now to the mound of blankets lying against the earth, and he lifted the corner of one of them, smiling with satisfaction. Virginia Whitechapel had come up beside her husband, and now she gripped his arm.

"Magnificent. By God, that's something!"

Whitechapel was looking down into the dead face of a Cheyenne medicine man. On his head was an elaborate feather-and-horn headdress, around his neck were six necklaces of turquoise, silver, bear claws, and elk teeth. His chest was covered with a highly decorated beaded vest, and wrapped around his mummified form was a magnificent white buffalo robe.

"You see here," Twelve Sky said, pointing to his dead father-in-law's hands. "This medicine bag, this medicine rattle."

"Yes, it is all marvelous. Look, Virginia, his face is still painted. Farnsworth, quickly! Load this onto the wagon."

"You like?"

"I am very pleased. The exchange is a costly one, Twelve Sky, but you fulfilled your end of the bargain. Take the guns and enjoy them." Whitechapel watched as the dead medicine man was loaded onto the wagon bed and covered over with a tarpaulin.

"More things. You want, I have," Twelve Sky said. Then, looking around, he moved stealthily to his horse mounting with the guncases still firmly in his hands.

"By God, we'll set London on its ear!" Whitechapel said after the Cheyenne were out of sight. "Rutledge Museum, indeed! They'll call it the Whitechapel Museum after this!"

seventeen _____

The long column was visible for miles across the prairie, the dust rising in wide-spreading, cinnamon-colored fans from the wheels of the wagons, the hooves of the horses and oxen.

"They're coming in," Private Wheeler shouted down from the wall, and Trueblood took off for the orderly room to deliver the message to Captain Conway.

"Coming in, Sergeant Olsen." Trueblood winked and closed the orderly room door. Gus, sighing with relief, got to his feet and went to the captain's office door.

Windy Mandalian, just in from a northern patrol with Mister Taylor, was in the captain's office, discussing the failure of the party to find any sign of Shell Eye. He had a glass of good whiskey in his hand and he nodded amiably to Gus Olsen.

"Lord Whitechapel's party is coming in, sir," Gus

said, eyeing Mandalian's glass enviously.

"Thank you, Gus," the captain said. "Any sign of trouble?"

"None at all, sir. Seems we've kept our English Lord alive and well. Happy, I hope."

"Fine." Conway allowed himself a smile. He finished his own drink and rose. "Want to have a look, Windy?"

"Yes, I do," Mandalian drawled. "Want to see if he's the hunter Gore and some of them other Englishmen were."

They went out into the harsh morning sunlight, Gus Olsen behind them. On the rampart Wheeler was pointing unnecessarily toward the incoming party.

"Travels light, don't he," Windy said dryly.

They stood watching for fifteen minutes until the wagons broke away from the post and lined out toward the river. Kincaid and Cohen, followed by the rest of the Easy Company men, rode in through the gate.

Kincaid grinned, saluted and stepped down. Conway walked to him. "Welcome back, Matt." He gripped Kincaid's shoulder and said, "No casualties, I hope?"

"No, sir, none," Kincaid replied.

"And no untoward incidents?"

"None, sir. His Lordship and party are intact, well, and happy, I believe. He fired a lot of ammunition, took a ton of trophies and I think he enjoyed his excursion."

"Fine." Conway turned to Cohen. "Welcome back, Ben. Had enough of that roving life?"

"For a time, sir. Definitely."

Whitechapel himself had not come into the outpost. Conway waited another few minutes and then shrugged and said, "Shall we retire to my office, gentlemen? I am sure we would all be interested to hear Lieutenant Kincaid's report."

"Mind if I saunter over and have a look at the trophies,

170

sir?" Windy asked. "I'd like to see if he truly does have something record size."

"As you like, Windy," Conway answered. The captain turned, put his arm around Kincaid's shoulder, and with Cohen and Olsen in tow, they walked back toward the orderly room.

Mandalian headed down toward the creek, where Whitechapel's people were setting up camp already. He ran into Tom Travers, a Coloradan he had once winter-camped with and who was now a wrangler for Lord Whitechapel, and they jawed awhile.

Leaving Travers, Windy walked around the camp, finding the wagons loaded with trophies. He saw one grizzly head that was massive enough to match anything Mandalian himself had ever seen, as well as scores of magnificent elk racks, and he was shown a cougar hide that looked large enough to cover a horse.

"What've you got over there?" he asked the camp hand.

"Dunno." The man scratched his head. "Never saw that."

With Windy behind him, the worker went to the wagon and lifted the tarp. "Holy Jesus," the man breathed.

"What?"

"Have a look. Now what in hell do you think that is? Never seen such a thing."

"I have," Windy said, his mouth forming a straight, harsh line. "What it is, is trouble."

Kincaid had nearly finished his report when Mandalian burst into the captain's office.

"Beggin' your pardon, Captain," the scout said, "but I've just come across something that figures to be bad trouble. Real bad."

"What?" Conway frowned in puzzlement. The man in buckskins looked worried, and it wasn't often that one

171

saw Windy Mandalian worried. He had seen too much to fly off the handle at every little thing.

Windy told them exactly what he had seen. "It has to be Sun Warrior's body, sir. And that's big trouble. Somehow that Englishman has got hold of Sun Warrior's remains. He was a holy man, sir. The Cheyenne can't let this go by. If they know about it, they'll come after it."

"How in hell . . . Matt, what do you know about this?"

"Twelve Sky," Kincaid said softly.

"What?"

"Twelve Sky, did you say, Matt?" Mandalian asked. At Kincaid's nod, Windy went on, "Twelve Sky is Sun Warrior's son-in-law, sir. A rascal and a wheeler-dealer, a real slippery man who'd sell anything—even his father-in-law's body, it seems."

"But what in God's name does Whitechapel want with such a thing!" Conway asked.

"He's a patron to some sort of museum, sir," Kincaid answered. "He's got a rivalry going with a Lord Bertram and they seem to spend a lot of time and money combing the far countries for relics to top each other."

"Well, he's got the topper this time," Conway said stiffly. "Any chance the Cheyenne can track Sun Warrior's remains here, Windy?"

"Sir, you know as well as I do that they can track anything anywhere. Yes, they'll read the sign and know exactly what's happened. If we're real lucky, maybe they won't happen to notice that Sun Warrior's burial site has been disturbed until Lord Whitechapel's gone."

It was a weak hope. Private Trueblood was again at the captain's doorway, and he came in, looking pale and drawn. "Sir—we've got visitors. Looks like five hundred hostiles out there, and they've got their paint on."

Conway snatched his hat and gunbelt from the coat tree and started toward the door. In the orderly room,

Cohen and Gus Olsen were already in motion. Outside on the parade there was a bustle of activity as the English party made for the gates, bringing their wagons with them. A quarter of a mile off, sitting their ponies in a long wavering line, was the Cheyenne war party.

Trueblood hadn't exaggerated. There were easily five hundred of them, and Conway swallowed a curse. "Ben, see that the walls are fully manned. Form up a bucket brigade and get the mess ready to receive wounded. Full preparations."

"War! Is it a war?" Lady Whitechapel asked excitedly.

It was not Virginia that Conway was interested in, but her husband. He found Lord Whitechapel among a group of his men, loading a big-bored Westley Richards rifle.

He looked up, and seeing Conway, Whitechapel said, "We're ready to stand with you, Captain, ready for a fight."

"By God, *I'm* not," Conway said loudly enough for his voice to echo all across the parade, where men were rushing toward the wall, loading guns, pulling on their trousers on the run. "This is your war, Whitechapel. I want you to go out there and put out the fire."

"Do you realize whom you are addressing, sir?" Whitechapel said, pulling himself up to his full height.

"I do. A fool." Conway spat out the words, knowing that this was liable to come back and land on his head. No matter—he wasn't going to have Easy Company involved in a battle of this size for nothing.

Whitechapel was sputtering away, growing red in the face, and Conway could see his next promotion winging away. Still, he had to lay it on the line.

"Lord Whitechapel, I have to explain something to you. In case you do not realize exactly why those Indians are out there wanting all of our scalps, it is because of something you engineered."

173

"Preposterous!"

"Far from it. You have committed a sacrilegious act, sir. You have become a grave robber. Twelve Sky, a perfect scoundrel, came to you and offered you a rare trophy to take back to England—"

"Yes, but—"

"But nothing, sir! You have stolen the remains of a Cheyenne legend. Pursuing a rather childish enthusiasm, spurred on by a desire to win some competition you apparently enjoy, you have stooped to dealing with criminals."

"Sir, I will take no more from you! Not one word more. A savage came, offering a bargain. I accepted it. If they have a complaint, let them settle it with this Twelve Sky."

"I imagine they already have," Conway said. The captain was rapidly losing all composure. Kincaid had a try at it.

"Sir, I wish you would try to see this from their perspective. What you have taken is not an old robe, the remains of a dead man. What you have taken are objects of reverence, objects of deep significance. It is very much as if the Indians had raided Westminister Abbey and taken the bones of your poets, or broken into your own family crypt and taken your father's remains. It is something that is not done! It is a crime in their eyes and, I must say, sir, in mine as well."

Whitechapel's face was still red, but slowly it blanched, the blood draining away. He lifted a trembling finger and lowered it again.

"You're right," he said finally, his voice papery, dry. "I was not considering that at all. You speak with perfect logic, sir. Forgive me, I've been a damned fool." Whitechapel shook his head heavily. "Send someone out there.

174

Tell them I'm returning Sun Warrior's remains. Tell them I was ignorant of their ways and I apologize."

With that, Whitechapel turned away and walked from them. The admission hadn't been easy for him to make, Conway realized. "Windy!" he called out. "Want to make powwow with those Cheyenne?"

"Will do, though I'm not eager. Hold this rifle, will you, Ben? I don't want them to get any ideas."

Mandalian stepped into the saddle of his appaloosa and rode out through the open gate. They saw him ride toward the Cheyenne, holding his right hand high. Along the parapet, Easy Company watched uneasily, damp palms gripping Springfields, eyes squinting into the sun, blood pounding.

It was over in minutes. Mandalian turned and came on in. "All they want's Sun Warrior's remains, sir," Windy told Captain Conway. "They know it would be big war to try to take them."

"They will be returned, Windy. Gus?"

"I'll drive the wagon out, sir."

Olsen's jaw was set as he walked to the wagon that held the body of Sun Warrior. He clambered aboard, unwound the reins from the brake handle, and started the team out onto the plains as Conway stood watching.

"I guess this has cost me my Rigby," Whitechapel said to his wife. "But a man is never too old to learn, and I suppose I've learned something."

Virginia, to her own surprise and Lord Whitechapel's pleasure, turned and hugged him, smiling up at him with the slightest hint of a tear in her eye.

"Wish the bastards would've tried it."

Heads along the parapet turned incredulously.

"That's a stupid thing to say, Fremont," Andy Pet-

tigrew said. "You wish they would have tried it! Goddamn, there'd be a few less of us here tomorrow if they
had tried it."

"You couldn't bring yourself to shoot one anway,
could you, Pettigrew? You and your Indian-lovin' ways.
You and your—"

Andy Pettigrew had kept it bottled up, but he was
hurting inside. He was going to lose Dawn Fox, and he
knew it. There had always been this idiot Fremont goad-
ing him, needling him, but Andy had managed to keep
it pretty well under control. Just now he couldn't take
any more.

He roared savagely and leaped on Fremont. Together
they fell from the wall, landing with a bone-cracking,
breathtaking jolt.

Conway's head came around. Cohen had already
started toward them. Along the wall a cheer went up.
Andy Pettigrew was astride Fremont, and his fists, right
and left, were falling savagely. Fremont's head was
slammed from side to side as Andy, in a mindless fury,
fought back against all the injustices heaped upon him
in the last few weeks.

"All right, all right!" It was Ben Cohen. He grabbed
Andy by his arms and lifted him from Fremont as if he
were a child. "That's it! Report to me in the morning. I
don't give a damn if you've got only two weeks left to
serve, Pettigrew. By God, you'll serve them like a soldier!"

"Excuse me." The lady touched Malone's arm and he
turned to find Virginia Whitechapel looking intently first
at Malone and then at the brawling soldiers. "What is
all of this? They are friends. They beat each other up?"

"They're not friends, Lady Whitechapel. Not exactly." Malone went on to tell the lady what had happened

176

between Fremont and Pettigrew. He related it all: the wild horses captured for Dawn Fox's father, the theft of those mustangs, the hopelessness Pettigrew must be feeling just now, a hopelessness that had blossomed into rage at one last jibe from Fremont.

"It is very sad," Lady Whitechapel said. "And very romantic."

"Yeah, it's romantic."

"Will you do something for me, Private Malone?"

"Ma'am?"

"Please tell your friend that he may have ten of my husband's horses." She smiled wistfully. "I too have always been a romantic." Then she turned and walked slowly away, leaving Malone to scratch his head before he realized what she had said and took off at a dead run to find Pettigrew.

Come morning, the Cheyenne had gone, taking with them the body of Sun Warrior. His Lordship, having had enough of Wyoming to last him a while, was watching as his wagons were prepared for the long journey back to Laramie. Andy Pettigrew had been over to Tipi Town at first light and returned with the hardly surprising news that he was going to marry Dawn Fox that evening. It was an occasion for celebration, and Malone had started early.

Behind the outpost he sat in the sunshine, resting his weary bones. In his hand was a bottle of whiskey, and if Cohen wanted to chew him out for it, so be it—he wanted it, needed it, was enjoying it.

The day was perfect, clear and bright and peaceful.

Until the tall Englishman in the dark suit appeared out of nowhere.

"Malone," he said, and Malone sighed, shaking his head heavily.

"It can't be you, Dolittle." But peering up with one red eye he saw that it was indeed Reginald Dolittle, the kitchen boss.

"I say, old man, hope there is no grudge held. I was only trying to execute my duties."

"Sure," Malone grumbled. "All right. Goodbye. Hope you get back to England all right." Malone waved a weary hand.

"There was one more thing I was hoping to do before leaving Wyoming," Dolittle said. Malone took a swig of the whiskey and peered up at the Englishman.

"What's that?"

"I know it's a savage superstition. Still, I'd like to make a wish."

"Huh?" Malone shook his head, trying to clear it. Slowly it dawned and a small beacon began to glow brightly in the back of his brain. "The Cheyenne wishing well!"

"Exactly." Dolittle clasped his hands behind his back and stood rocking on his heels. "I see you've made some improvements. A tent pitched over the well."

Malone looked around. There was no one in sight. "You have to protect it, you know. From the rain and all," he said.

"Certainly."

Malone got to his feet, tucking the bottle behind his belt. He threw an arm around Dolittle's shoulders. "Want to have a closer look?"

"I'd be very obliged, really."

"All right." Dolittle found Malone's manner friendly. He had thought the American might still be angry. He was glad to see it wasn't so. Malone led him to the wishing well, which was now concealed by a low tent.

"Is it all right to go in?"

"Quite all right," Malone said, politely holding back

178

the tent flap. Dolittle strode past him, stepping into the latrine, and Malone stuck his foot out.

Dolittle hollered and toppled forward. The ensuing splash was deep and satisfying. The Englishman's voice rose furiously.

"Damn you, you . . . Irishman! You're filthy! Filthy. This is no wishing well!"

"I dunno." Malone took a long pull at his bottle and gazed toward the blue skies over Wyoming. "I got my wish."

Watch for

EASY COMPANY
AND THE GYPSY RIDERS

twenty-ninth novel in
the exciting EASY COMPANY series

Coming in June!

EASY COMPANY

MORE ROUGH RIDING ACTION FROM JOHN WESLEY HOWARD